ANOTHER WORLD ANOTHER PLACE

ISBN: 978-1-963565-16-4 (Paperback)

Library of Congress Control Number: 2024906016

Printed in the United States of America

Published by

info@thequippyquill.com
(302) 295-2278

CONTENTS

THE REIGN OF A YOUNG QUEEN 1

ANOTHER WORLD, ANOTHER PLACE 12

IN ALL THESE YEARS 24

JOURNEY TO THIS PLACE CALLED EARTH 38

STILL ON THE THRONE 47

ALL THE QUEEN'S MEN 55

THE GIFT 62

"ONCE THE QUEEN, ALWAYS THE QUEEN" 71

    (A War Begins) 71

"THE SECRET AFFAIR" 77

SECOND CHAPTER 85

"INTO THE VALLEY OF PEACE" 86

OUT OF THE VALLEY OF PEACE 94

ABOUT THE AUTHOR 108

THE REIGN OF A YOUNG QUEEN

King Alijal sat by the bedside of his wife Queen Equilla. She lay in bed, ill of pneumonia. He held her hand as she closed her eyes to go to sleep. It was time for him to turn in for the night, but Alijal couldn't go to sleep knowing his wife was dying. He prayed for a little while then he lied down next to his Queen. Alijal opened his eyes to a bright sunny morning. He touched his wife's arm, and she was cold as ice. He knew then she was gone.

Equilla laid there in peace and beauty. Alijal stared at her as the sun shined upon her face. It was as if she was only sleeping. Recently Equilla told Alijal she wasn't feeling well and was ready to meet the maker. He certainly wasn't ready for her to leave him.

Alijal put together a memorial service at a beautiful funeral home for Queen Equilla four days later. A huge crowd of people came to pay their respects to their Queen. Before the service started and the people arrived, Alijal viewed the setting, he was amazed. Seventy- five lit candles which counted every year of her life. He stood over her body while she laid beautifully in her casket. When the service began, everyone drowned in their tears. Alijal refused to cry. His wife wasn't suffering no more and that's all that mattered but his heart was starting to break because he was alone now. When he finally buried his beloved wife, Alijal shed his tears when he alone in their bedroom. His heart began aching again so he got on his knees and prayed that he wouldn't die of a broken heart. He wanted to sleep peacefully and wake up to new day, knowing that everything is going to be alright.

Alijal was woken up by a knock at his door. "Come in." Harper the harp man entered. "Good morning your majesty. I know this is your time of grieving, but I thought it would be nice if you heard a song to brighten your day." "I'd love to hear a song," Alijal said. Harper began playing the angelic sounds of his harp. Alijal was sitting up in bed, but he leaned back against the headboard, closing his eyes. His mind was put at ease, but Equilla would pop back in his head. Whenever he sits on the throne, she won't be there next to him. Whenever he's in bed, she's not next to him to keep him warm. He can't live alone and Equilla's not coming back. Maybe I can find a new Queen. His eyes shot open. "A new Queen!" he said aloud. Harper stopped playing. "You okay sire?" "Guard!" Alijal called. The guard standing in the hallway, came. "Find Wallace for me." "Yes, your majesty," the guard said. "What's going on sire?" Harper asked. "I want to send a message to all the single women. A man like me shouldn't have to live his life alone." Wallace came a few moments later. "You needed me sire?" "Yes, I want you to make some flyers saying that the King would like for every single lady in Sedonia to meet with him. Women only between the ages of 20-30." Wallace, Harper, and guard all looked at each other wondering why Alijal wanted a new wife so soon and so young. Alijal was almost eighty years old. "Let's get to it," the King said to Wallace. They dared not ask why. Wallace got to work on the flyers. "I wish to be alone so I can begin my day." The guard and Harper left the King's room.

Alijal began his meetings for a new bride on a Saturday afternoon in the dining room. He was only expecting a small group of women to show up, instead thousands showed up. He thinks some didn't read the flyers correctly, "single women." Some women showed up with husbands or their significant other. Some of the interviews, Alijal have done, he noticed certain ones didn't have what it took to be a leader. They just want to live the life of luxury. There was a woman named Veelola whom her husband, Lathus called her Veel. Something didn't seem right about either one of them when they walked into the room. Alijal didn't speak with Veel very long. The interviews lasted the entire day and he didn't find what he was looking for. "Try again," Mel the head of the guards, told him. "Set up some more meetings next weekend. You're bound to find somebody." "I can't go on like this," Alijal said. "Like what, sire?" "Being alone." "We're all here for you. I know it's not the same as having a spouse by your side, but you should never feel alone." "Mel you've always been a great friend and a great person. I know there's a Queen out there." That night and the next couple of nights, Alijal had a hard time sleeping. He kept looking on the other side of the bed, imagining Equilla there. Out of one of those nights he'd be lying in bed, reaching in the air thinking Equilla would fall from heaven into his arms. Now he's telling himself to stop hoping, stop dreaming.

Time keeps going by. Another day of teaching art and science at Cyon Junior High was over for young woman named Sylvia Soom. She was about to leave her empty classroom, when another teacher and a friend of hers named Magalina stopped her. "He's still looking for a bride." Her friend handed her a flyer. "Not this again," Sylvia said. "You need to see this man," Magalina said. "You have what it takes to be a wife. This is no ordinary man… he wants a Queen." "I don't have what it takes to be royalty." "How do you know? Sylvia, you need to be with somebody. You're well organized and have it together. Just go see what he's talking about." "I don't know. I find it strange that he's looking for a new wife when his wife just died less than two weeks ago." "Maybe he doesn't want to be alone," Magalina said. "I have to think about this." "Don't think, do."

Alijal met with more young women on another Saturday. It was smaller group this time, but he wasn't sure about the few women. He didn't think any of them would make a great wife. "Is there anyone else in the hallway?" Alijal asked Mel. Mel went out in the hallway. A lady had just gotten there. "Any more ladies coming?" Mel asked her. "I think I'm the only one," she said. Sylvia entered the dining room. Alijal was sitting at the table. He greeted her with a smile. "Please have a seat." She sits across from him. "So how are you Miss…" "Sylvia Soom," she ended. "What do you do for a living, Miss Soom?" "I'm an art teacher and I teach science." "Oh, an artist, I love art. You like being a teacher?" "A whole lot." "How would you feel if you had to give up teaching and become a King's wife?" "I don't know what to say. I'd never imagined myself becoming royalty. I have a question for you your majesty… how come a man your age wants a wife so young?" "Me and my wife Equilla never had children. Now that she's gone, I thought it would be wise to bring someone young in to take my place and the late Queen's place." "Am I really the right choice?" "Definitely. I knew when you walked through the door. The thousands of women I've talked to just wanted to impress me by their appearance. You're just being you. I would like to come to your school. I want to check out all the fabulous artwork." "That would be great," Sylvia said. "I'll see you in a couple of days, Miss Soom." "You think I've found the right one?" Alijal asked Mel, after she left. "She is divine," Mel said.

Sylvia was teaching her art class on a Monday afternoon. The principal came to her door and said, "you have a visitor." "Hello your majesty," Sylvia said. Her students dropped their paintbrushes when they saw Alijal. The King has never come to the school before. "Everyone, this King Alijal." "Hello!" the class said. "Hello everyone," he said back. "Alijal is going to sit and watch what we're working on." He stayed for an hour, then he was escorted by his security guards to his car. Alijal called Sylvia later in the evening. "You have any plans this Saturday?" "No, not really." "I want you to paint me a picture." "Okay, a picture of what?" Sylvia asked. "I'll let you know when I see you again and maybe we should have dinner." "That would be nice." "How about eleven?" he asked. "Eleven o' clock will be great." "I'll see you Saturday at eleven," Alijal said.

Sylvia began painting a picture of Alijal in the pinkish background of the ocean, sky and the sparkling sands as he stood there in his royal attire. It was lots of people there at the beach that afternoon. She wasn't too sure about painting the picture of the King because Sylvia was afraid it wouldn't look like him, but she did her best. After they left the beach, they were driven back to palace. He gave her a tour of his home. "What do you think?" Alijal asked. "This is a magnificent place you have." "Thank you. You must be hungry. It's time for that dinner I promised you." They had their little fancy feast in the dining room where they had first met. "Is this lifestyle still something you would want? It is a great responsibility other than the extravagant environment." Alijal chewed on a slice of ham and continued. "I know I want to share all this with you." He showed her a beautiful ring, he took out of a little box. "I'll give it a try," Sylvia said. He took her by the hand and put the ring on her finger. "Then it's settled," he said.

"I am so jealous," Magalina said, when Sylvia showed the ring to her at work. "You went to meet the King now you're about to become the Queen. See, you got lucky. I knew you would attract a wealthy man." "This wasn't luck and I've never been the one to marry a man for his money. I love the life I've been living. I'm choosing to take this step." "I'm happy you chose this step," Magalina said.

The nineties were coming to an end and a new century was approaching. A big wedding was being planned and the entire kingdom was excited. Sylvia was a unique-minded person. She wanted the colors for her wedding to be pink and silver. The beverage that's going to be served at the reception is going to be pink champagne. She wanted her wedding dress to be a carnation pink but none of the bridal places had any wedding dresses in pink, so she picked a dress that was her style and she dyed it pink. The wedding date was supposed to be set for the first day of spring, but since it was about to be a new year, Alijal and Sylvia both agreed to get married on New Year's Eve. Magalina was helping her in her wedding dress on the big day and Magalina started crying. "I can't believe my best friend is getting married." "I can't believe it either," Sylvia said, "I'm also nervous." "You have nothing to be nervous about." They hugged each other. When it was time for time for Miss Soom to walk down the aisle, she couldn't believe the huge crowd and how lovely the place looked. That long journey down the aisle had her thinking about the transition she was about to make. Seeing Alijal standing there, waiting, all dressed in silver, next to the priest, made her realize how real this was. When she finally came face to face with the King at the altar, Sylvia thought about how it would be making love to an eighty-year-old man, even though he didn't look bad for his age. As the ceremony began, she kept thinking how, does he really feel about her. He made her feel good, inside. She looked up to him. They held hands and looked into each other's eyes as the priest continued. They said their "I do's" and then Alijal kissed the bride. The way he kissed her wasn't just some kiss. It was the first time they ever kissed, and it was different from any other kiss she's had in her life. Then they turned to the crowd. "Alijal shouted, "meet your new Queen!" The people stood up and made lots of noise. Harper walked up to Sylvia and said, "Your crown my Queen." He carried a beautiful crown on a pillow. She took the crown and placed it on her head. Everyone feasted in the dining hall for the reception. After everyone went home, Alijal and Sylvia packed up for their honeymoon. They headed to their hotel suite that was seven miles from the palace. It sat on beach and the scenery was different. The sky and ocean were bluish-green, the sand was sparkling sandy brown. Alijal and Sylvia stayed in their room while everyone all over Sedonia began celebrating the coming of a new century. Sylvia had on her robe, brushing her shoulder length hair in the bathroom. Then she left the bathroom to stand out on the balcony. She loved the breeze and the excitement of the people down below. She couldn't see the ocean because it was night now but the sound of the waves were, like music to her ears. Alijal had went to the bathroom after she came out. He's been unpacking once they got there. While she was still enjoying the sounds of the waves, Alijal came up behind her and showed her a painting. A painting of her. Sylvia was without words at first. "Did you do this?" "Yes, I can paint too. I wanted to wait 'til this night to show you." "It's wonderful. It looks just like me." "My lovely Queen." He had the look of love in his eyes. "Five, four, three, two, one… Happy New Year's!" the people on the beach shouted. Fireworks colored the sky up like a rainbow. The people partied, drank, and kissed. The King and Queen celebrated their New Year with just a kiss. They returned to the palace after three days on their honeymoon. Sylvia was ready to start her new life. Alijal had a tailor bring in fancy gowns and other royal attire for her to wear. Sylvia thought, being a Queen was going to be a tough job at first. It was nothing but looking fabulous and sitting on a throne. Which was great but the thing that wasn't great to her was not having to anything for yourself. She liked doing things for herself. Sedonia was such a peaceful world. There were never no wars. The Kings and Queens over the centuries, were very strict on the way everyone was supposed to live. If you didn't follow the rules, you were put away or forced to leave Sedonia. The same rules still apply today. Alijal was a great husband to Sylvia but she didn't understand why he wanted to sleep in separate rooms. This arrangement has been like this since they've come back from their honeymoon. Two weeks of living in the palace, there's been a couple of nights Sylvia walked past Ailjal's room and heard him shout "Equilla!" The way he's been eating was unhealthy. She knew he didn't make it to eighty by eating like that. Sylvia wondered was this really the right path for her. She went through many months of this and Sylvia decided she didn't want to be here anymore. She went in her room and started packing some of her things. Then thoughts came in her head. I can't just up and leave. That would be disrespectful. But I don't want to stay here if he wants to still dream about his first wife. That's why he makes me sleep in a separate room. We haven't shared a bed since the honeymoon. People are willing to do things for you when you've the boss or a leader because they're getting paid good, I like people who do things because they want to do it. Sylvia became hesitate about leaving. Someone knocked at her door. "Come in." "Your majesty, the King is ill, you must hurry!" Mel told her. They hurried to Alijal's room. He was lying on his bed barely breathing. "Has anyone called the doctor?" Sylvia asked. "Yes, he's on his way." The doctor came quickly. The doctor put him on oxygen, checked his pressure, and drew some blood from him. Alijal was able to sleep a few moments later. "I should have the test results in a week," the doctor said. "Will he be alright?" Sylvia asked. "Yes, but I have to ask you is he eating a lot of salty, fatty foods?" "He has been eating unhealthy," she said. "Well, he cannot eat like that. His blood pressure was pretty high. If he keeps on eating like this, he'll have a massive heart attack and die. Have a good day." "Thank you, doctor." Sylvia gently touched Alijal's hand. He still slept. Then she left his room right after the doctor had left. Sylvia went back to her room and took her clothes out of her suitcase. She walked around in the palace to have more time to think. She thought she knew the palace, but Sylvia came to an area of her home, she'd never been. There was a door that lead to somewhere or kept secret. Sylvia was curious about what was behind this door. Maybe I shouldn't, she thought. But I'm the Queen. I should know everything about this place. She was afraid to open it, but she did. When she opened the door, she couldn't believe what she saw. It was like an enchanting garden, a huge bed of roses. There was no ceiling above. It was a mild day and the wind was blowing. Well, she thought there was wind blowing. It began sounding like someone singing. She didn't see anybody. Then some heavenly like beings appeared that looked like women floating around. One of the angels smiled at her. Sylvia smiled back. "This is magnificent," Sylvia said. "Your majesty," someone called from the hallway. She got out of there quickly. Sylvia made sure she shut the door. "Your majesty, I was checking on you, seeing if you were okay," Mel said. "I'm fine, nothing to worry about."

Alijal obeyed the doctor's orders for a month but went back to his poor eating habits. He stuck to salads, baked chicken and drinking diet sodas within that month. Alijal couldn't take eating like that much more so he ordered the chefs to cook what he really wanted. Sylvia noticed during his dieting process he lost a little weight, but she also noticed when he didn't eat properly because his skin broke out and he gained extra weight. There were also times he was throwing up in the bathroom. So, Sylvia chose to start cooking his meals. She told the chefs to no longer feed him. The first day of the change, Alijal got up in the morning, expecting hotcakes, buttered biscuits and cheese omelets. It was a note sitting on the dining room table saying, "This is your breakfast." Right next to the note was a plate of rice cakes, three slices of ham, sunny side up eggs and an unsweetened iced tea. "What the heck?" he said. Sylvia came in. "Yes, I cooked your breakfast and I'll do the same for lunch and dinner from here on out. You won't watch how you eat so I'm going to make sure you do eat right. "Why won't you people leave me alone and let me die! "I'm your wife and I want you to live!" He left. His health issues changed him so much. The kind King has become a grumpy King. He wasn't going along with the strict diet routine. She made lunch for him, but it sat on the table getting cold. He told Wallace and Mel to get some McDonald's for him. Alijal hid in his bedroom to eat his Quarter pounder and fries. About six that evening, he got hungry again and went to the kitchen. The chefs Amu and Lunia were about finished with dinner. "Smells good guys, what's for dinner?" "Sirloin steak smothered in sautéed onions," Lunia said. "I can't hardly wait," Alijal said. "Your majesty," Amu began, "the Queen said she has your dinner being prepared." "What did she make for me?" "I made boiled shrimp, steamed broccoli and bread sticks for you," Sylvia said, when she walked in the kitchen. "You're not trying to feed me; you're trying to starve me with this low-calorie stuff." "You just had McDonald's today," she said. "How did you know? Did Wallace tell you or was it Mel? I hope it wasn't Mel. He's supposed to be my boy. Me and him might have a talk." "It's for your own good." "Look I am the King here! I will eat whatever I please. All of you are eating all this high cholesterol food and none of you are getting any younger. I am a man of eighty years old. I've took care of my health all these years. And Sylvia since you seem to be such a caring wife, you should be caring about satisfying my stomach. Being on an extreme diet has made my stomach growl half the time and I be thinking my stomach is trying to have a conversation with me. So, if you people don't mind, I'm going to wash my hands for dinner, sirloin steak is on the menu." The doctor has been making his visits to see how well Alijal's health was holding up. Alijal's been getting good results. As long as the doctor was telling them good news, Sylvia didn't worry about how he ate. She couldn't anyway. He said it loud and clear that he was going to eat what he wanted. Alijal lived his life. When he leaves this world, she will be the one ruler. The question is, will she be ready when the time comes?

One night, Sylvia walked past Alijal's bedroom on the way to the kitchen to get a glass of water. His door was open, and a guard was standing out in the hallway by his door. It sounded like Alijal was sobbing. She wanted to go in to see if he was alright but she knew the guard was there to keep her from entering. Alijal knows Sylvia passes by his bedroom every other night. Most of the time he keeps the door shut. Many months have passed and Alijal has fallen into depression. At times Sylvia would ask, "what's wrong?" But he would never answer. Every time they ate together, he'll eat small bites at a time, making little conversation. Sylvia's very worried but there's nothing she can do since he won't tell her anything. He even looked like he aged another ten years. She wanted to call the doctor in but Alijal told her no. "This is it for me. My days are numbered." She wished he wouldn't say things like that. When Thanksgiving and Christmas came around, Alijal and Sylvia had their family members feast with them. They had so much food, it could last them until the next year. Sylvia uses to be worried about how Alijal ate now she's worried that he doesn't eat enough. He's become quite thin.

His family is even questioning what's going on with him. He wouldn't answer them instead he'll say, "we're supposed to be enjoying the holidays." Everyone did enjoy the holidays. After Christmas passed, Alijal stayed in bed, never left his room. He did the same thing days after. The chefs would bring food to his room, but he wouldn't eat it. On New Year's Eve, all the people of Sedonia and everyone in the palace was preparing to celebrate, that evening. King Alijal was very sick and very weak. No one was allowed in his room until the early evening he had one the guards bring Sylvia to him. "You wanted me?" she asked. She hated seeing him like this. "Yes, will you keep me company." Sylvia pulled up a chair next to his bed. She held his hand. It was very bony not like it used to be, strong and masculine. "Why won't you let me take care of you?" Sylvia asked. "I don't want to be saved," he said. Alijal was looking her over. "You look lovely. Did you wear that dress for me?" "It's for the New Year's Eve party that's about to begin in another hour. The palace is going to be packed tonight. I arranged for the biggest party to be here. "That's nice but will you spend a little time with me?" he asked. "I'll be back in a little while. The guests will be coming soon, and I want to greet them." Sylvia heads to the throne room where the event was taking place and she was ready for the guest to arrive. Everything was setup and ready. Seven o' clock, many couples arrived, and Sylvia greeted them at the door. Eight o' clock, small groups of people arrived, Sylvia greeted them also. By nine o' clock, people were constantly coming in every minute. Everyone was enjoying the food and music and Sylvia was pleased with everything, but it got so crowded by ten o' clock it wasn't much room to dance. She was so caught up with what everyone else was doing, she forgot about Alijal until he popped up in her head. "Oh, no Alijal!" She hurried to his room. "Alijal." She knelt down by his bedside and touched his hand. Alijal opened his eyes and looked at her. "I didn't mean to forget about you. It's so many people here. I was making sure everybody was catered to. What can I get for you, my King?" "I like a glass of water." "You want anything to eat?" "No, just a glass of water." When she went to leave, he said, "You do look lovely, my lovely Queen." She gave a quick smile and went to the kitchen for his water. She got a cold glass of water from the crystal-clear water dispenser. "Why are you in the kitchen? You should be out here dancing," Mel said. "Can't right now. I got to take Alijal some water. "Is he doing okay?" "Yeah, he wants me to keep him company… have fun." "I know I'm having fun," Mel said. Sylvia went back to Alijal's bedroom. She thought he was just resting his eyes again, so she lifted his head to help him drink his water and she knew he was too weak to hold the glass himself. His eyes remained closed and he didn't respond. "Alijal," she said. Sylvia got nervous. She laid his head back down on the pillow. Sylvia felt his neck. She felt nothing. Then she broke down. Sylvia laid her head on his chest knowing there wasn't going to be a heartbeat. She kept her head laid on his chest, hoping his heart was going to beat again. Sylvia continued to cry her heart out over her husband that was now gone. She could hear everybody partying from down the hall. She knew it was almost midnight, but she wasn't ready to show her face to the crowd. Sylvia wanted everyone to bring in the New Year with happiness. The countdown was on. It was now 2001. She laid next to her husband and stared at him with her watery eyes. The crowd got louder and was partying even more. Sylvia went to the bathroom to wash her face. She took one last look in the mirror to make sure her eyes weren't still red. She was trying to ease her way through the crowd, looking for Mel. She wasn't going to try too hard. It was too massive of a crowd to find him. She went to the kitchen for a drink. She ended up finding him in there pouring himself a drink. "How about that dance?" he asked. "Mel, Alijal just died." Mel didn't know what to say. "Are you serious?" "Yes." Mel left the kitchen. Sylvia followed him. He pushed his way through the crowd to get to the DJ. Mel whispered in the DJ's ear. The DJ stopped the music. Everyone wondered why the music stopped. "Sorry about stopping the party, but I have some terrible news… King Alijal just died," Mel said. The people were shocked and some started crying. "I know this has suddenly become an unhappy moment, but we can still celebrate by remembering him." All the lights in the palace were turned off because some lit up their cell phones for like a vigil. Some stood in the hallway outside his bedroom in silence. The whole palace was silent. Everyone went home, knowing the King's death was going to have an impact on how the New Year was going to turn out.

Alijal's body was cremated and services for him was held three days later right in the throne room. The same great crowd of people that celebrated the New year, came back to pay respects to the King and mourn him. Once all the people went home, Sylvia shut herself off in her room. She didn't expect this moment to come this soon. She took a look out her window at the ocean from a distance. Many thoughts went through her head. Sylvia has now prepared herself for this responsibility for being a Queen who sits alone and the only ruler of this world… or she thought. Sylvia had found out during her outings and messages from Wallace, that ever since Alijal passed, a man named Lathus and a woman named Veel, claimed to be rulers of a certain part of Sedonia. The dark end or the dark side which was many miles from the palace and the rest of the world. And as time went by, Sylvia has learned that some women have become employed at some restaurants and strip clubs that Lathus hired men to build near his territory. What bothered her the most was the women served customers in nudity. Some of the young ladies were under eighteen. She knew this was a challenge and the first war this world was going to have. Sylvia maybe was the only real ruler, but she wasn't alone. As long as God was on her side, she was going to step up to the plate. So whatever evil came her way she was going to stand here and be waiting.

ANOTHER WORLD, ANOTHER PLACE

Nate Patricks, an astronaut from Long Beach, California was traveling alone in his spacecraft with his pet monkey, Chiha he brought from Australia. Ever since growing up, Nate has always believed there was life on another planet. During his journey, he spotted an object coming his direction. He knew it had to be a meteor, so he tried to swerve around it. But it was too late. The meteor hit his spacecraft and he was losing control and he couldn't get in contact with anyone. He tried to maneuver some place to land but there wasn't no place to land. All Nate could think that he was going to die so he just closed his eyes.

It was a cool breezy night when Sylvia was sitting in front of her bedroom mirror brushing her long hair. She gazed out her opened balcony door at the dark sky over the ocean. Sylvia could hear thunder. She shuts her window and gets ready for bed. All the guards were guarding all around her home and one guard standing outside of her bedroom like always. Sylvia turns off the light and lies down. She closes her eyes. Then she opens her eyes for a second. In that second, something comes crashing through her bedroom window. A beast with bloody red eyes, sharp teeth and fuzzy fur. Sylvia was sitting up in her bed, terrified. The beast was holding a tranquilizing gun. He speaks the words, "Long lives the Queen!" The beast shoots Sylvia in the chest with a tranquilizer. She falls on the floor into a coma- like sleep. The beast put Sylvia's body into a bag and they carry off into the night. The guard guarding outside of Sylvia's bedroom was asleep. Mel and the other guards came running. "Boy what are you doing asleep?" Mel asked, hitting the guard aside his head. "I heard the noise all way down the hall!" "I'm very sorry, sire," the guard said. "Sylvia!" Mel yells, beating on the door. There was no answer. They kicked in her bedroom door. They all discovered the shattered glass from the window and Sylvia's disappearance. Mel knew who might have took her, so he planned a mission to find her.

Morning. The sun has risen over the sparkling pink ocean. Nate opens his eyes. He looks at his hands and all over himself. A smile was upon his face. "I'm alive! I can't believe it!" He looks around and sees nothing but sand and water. Nate scoops up some of the sand in the palm of his hand. He stares at the sparkling crystal sand in his hand. Then he pours it back on the ground. Nate rubs his head feeling so confused. "Damn, where am I?" he asked himself. "Get off my beach!" someone said. "Who said that?" "Get off my beach!" someone said again. Nate looks around. He sees no one. He turns around and a sea gull was standing there. Nate jumps. "What the hell is going on?" Nate asked. "What are you doing on this beach?" the sea gull asked. "I don't know. I don't know where I am." "You're in Sedonia. I've never seen your kind before. The Queen will have to be notified about you." "What Queen?" Nate asked. "Queen Sylvia. The ruler of this world and this land." "I know I'm definitely not on Earth. We don't have talking sea gulls. The only animals we have that talk are parrots. Speaking of animals, I can't find my pet monkey." "Here I am," Chiha said, brushing her body off from the sand. "You can talk too?" Nate asked. "Of course, I can." She climbs on Nate's shoulder. "What I want to know is how did I get here… well I got here by spacecraft---- my spacecraft!" Nate saw that his spacecraft was lying in the sand, demolished. "That's just great. How am I going to get back to Earth?" "The only thing I can tell you is to go see the see the Queen, but you must beware of her guards because they're not very friendly." "Which direction is the Queen's place?" "Just right over those hills." Nate looks over the hills. He saw a huge palace and a beautiful city behind it. He turned around and saw that the sea gull had vanished. Boy this place is really weird. I feel like I'm in the land of OZ," Nate said. "I'm certainly not Toto," Chiha said. Nate and Chiha hurried over the hills. He was out of breath when he got to the palace. While he was trying to catch his breath about twenty soldiers surrounded him with their swords aimed at him. Mel steps forward. "Who goes there?" Mel asked. "Who the heck are you?" Nate asked. Nate's on his knees with hands up." "I'm Mel, the Queen's head guardian. Who might you be?" "I'm Nate Patricks. I'm an astronaut from the planet we call Earth." "So, you're an earthling. Is that what that USA stands for on your uniform?" "Yes, I'm from the United States of America." Mel had all the guards put away their weapons. "We thought you might have been someone who sent those beasts to kidnap Sylvia. They took her last night." "Do you know why they wanted to take her?" Nate asked. "To destroy her and to destroy us the people." Sylvia is our light, our inspiration. The beasts want us to die and this world to be in complete darkness. Without her there is no us." "This is terrible. I needed to see her about getting back home." "What is your world like?" Mel asked. "Well, it's a place where there's more evil than good… but life is what you make of it." "If you want love and happiness, this is the place. Why don't you and your furry friend come with me and I'll introduce you to my people." "Okay," Nate said. With Chiha on his shoulder, Nate follows Mel into the palace. The guards close the doors behind them. The people were standing around talking. They all stopped when they saw Mel, Nate, and Chiha. "Sir Mel, where is Sylvia?" a girl asked. "That's what I have to talk to everyone about… Sylvia has been kidnapped. "Oh my God, oh my God," everyone was saying. "It's going to be alright. We know where she is and will bring her back with the help of my noble man, Nate." The people drew close to Nate and Chiha. They were overwhelmed with them in their presence. Chubby, short man named Harper, looked Nate straight in the face and said," You are the great and noble one. I know you will bring back our Queen." "Yes, I will," Nate said. Nate turned to Mel. "So where is this place your Queen is kept?" "The dark side. A very long journey from here. It's going to be just us two, if you're still down." "You're not bringing the soldiers with us?" "No, they have to watch the palace because it must never be unguarded." "Hold up, wait a minute!" Wallace said, who had just walked in on their conversation. "Damn what does this lazy boy want?" Mel asked himself. "I know you're not planning on going somewhere without me?" Wallace asked. "As a matter of fact, I am because this is a job that only men can handle not something for a lazy boy like you." "Who are you calling lazy, softie?" "You." Wallace ignored Mel but then focused on Nate. Wallace looked at Nate up and down. "Who's this… your girlfriend?" Wallace asked Mel, laughing. "Get him, Nate," Chiha whispered to him. "I use, to date your mother," Nate said, "she didn't tell you about me?" Then Mel started laughing. Wallace was pissed. "The heck with you two. Neither one of you don't stand a chance against an army of evil in the dark side." "Look at you. You're not even dressed, and you come out here talking stuff to me and my man Nate. We're ready to go now." "I'm going back to the spa room to finish up my back massage and I'll be ready because you know you guys are going to need me." Wallace ran off. "He must don't know what NOW means. But he is right. We do need him. You never know what can happen," Mel said. "Follow me." "Are we leaving now?" Nate asked. "Not yet. I just need to hurry Wallace up." Wallace was getting his back massage in the spa room. Five women that worked in the spa room, gathered around Nate and Mel. "Hello Sir Mel, who's your friend?" one of the women asked. "This Nate and his furry friend--- Chiha!" Chiha finished for him." Nate wasn't paying attention to anything except the woman that was giving Wallace his massage. She and Nate were giving each other eye contact as she continued to massage Wallace's back. "Oh my, you're so handsome," the woman said to Nate, touching and rubbing him. "Would you like a back massage, or would you rather have a full body massage?" another woman asked. "I'd love a massage, but I really don't have the time," he answered. Mel stood over Wallace as he was enjoying his massage. "Excuse me, miss," Mel said to the woman, massaging Wallace. She ended the massage and left. "Hey, why did you stop?" Wallace asked, not knowing the woman left. "Wallace we are going to need you to come with us." "I knew you were going to need me… hey, were you trying to look at me?" Wallace asked. "I don't want to look at your ashy ass. You need to get dressed." All the women left the room. "So how are we getting to this place called the dark side?" Nate asked. "I have a great ride for a great journey," Mel said. Nate, Chiha, and Wallace follow Mel, outside. "Dane, this is a nice ride. It's those new whatchamacallits?" Nate asked. "This is a 2002 TAC to the Max," Mel answered. "What does TAC mean, tight ass car or something?" "I guess you can say that, but it could stand for a lot of things." "Most of the women here have some TAC," Wallace said. "Meaning?" Nate asked. "Don't you even say it," Wallace said. "All women are to you is sex objects." "Yeah, what else?" Wallace asked. "And how do you know what women have? None of them would lay with you if you were the last man on the planet." "That's what you think," Wallace said. "Forget I even said anything. Let's get going." "Before we get on the road, do you mind if I get something to eat because a brother is kind of hungry," Nate said. "There's a McDonald's a mile from here, we can go there," Mel said. They stopped at the McDonald's. "Welcome to McDonald's … may I take your order?" a girl asked, when they got to the counter. "Is it breakfast or lunch?" Mel asked. "Either or," the girl answered. "We'll have lunch, and this will be on the same ticket. I'll have a Big Mac meal with a Coca-Cola," Mel said. "I'll have a double quarter pounder meal with a Dr. Pepper," Nate said. "And for you sir?" the girl asked Wallace. "I'll have a Big Mac meal with a Sprite because I'm the Mack of the millennium." Wallace winked his eye and blew a kiss at her. She rolled her eyes at him and asked Mel, "Is there anything else for you?" "No that will be all." "Your total is eleven dollars and fifty cents." Nate pulls out his share of money. "I got it," Mel said. "Are you from somewhere else because I've never seen that type of money before?" the girl asked. "I'm from Earth, an American." "That's interesting," the girl said. Mel pulls out some silver coins and pays her. She presents their order to them and they find a place to sit. "I'm sure hating this. All the women want to have something against me ever since American man came along," Wallace said. "Women have always had something against you because how you approach them," Mel said. "Look who's talking. That's funny coming from somebody that's gay," Wallace said. "Gay!" Mel replied. "Yeah, everybody knows you're gay." "Let me tell you something, I like girls and only girls. I get respect from them because I show respect. Plus, I wear medals on my chest that stand for something. What do you have? Nothing. Because you're nothing but a message boy that sends the wrong message to women." "What! Wrong message!" Wallace replied. "At least I'm packing a lot in my pants and women like that." "Boy your stuff ain't no bigger than this." Mel holds up a French fry. Wallace became heated. "Fuck you, Mel. You don't know shit! Fuckin' faggot!" He jumps over the table and knocks Wallace on the floor. Then Mel pulls out his sword and holds it up to Wallace's throat. "You wanna call me a faggot." "That's what you are," Wallace said. "Oh, I'm a faggot but I was man enough to knock you on the floor and you're laying here looking like a bitch." "Come on now. You two need to quit. We are here on a mission to find Sylvia and are wasting time," Nate said. "You're the one that wanted to stop for some food," Wallace said. "So, what. Sylvia could be dying while you guys are fighting. So, we need to get on the ball." "That's telling them Nate," Chiha said, then eating a fry. Mel removes his sword away from Wallace's throat. "Let's finish our grub and get out of here," Mel said.

Late evening. It's been over thirteen hours of their journey. Chiha, Nate, and Mel were in the back seat fast asleep while Wallace was driving. They pass through an exotic part of the city. Wallace pulls in front of a club. All three of them wake up. "Where are we at?" Mel asked. "I want to get a drink," Wallace said. "This is not the time for a drink. We need to get to the dark side." "We are not going to make it to the dark side tonight because it's late and I'm getting tired. So, it be best we check into a motel." They all decide to go in the club. It was a tropical forest like place with palm trees and a crystal -clear fountain pool. The erotic dancers and cocktail waitresses were totally nude. Mel, Wallace, and Nate with Chiha perched on his shoulder, get seated. One of the waitresses come to their table. Her whole body was covered in glitter. "What can I get you gentlemen?" "I just want a coke and rum," Nate said. "I'll have a penis colada," Mel said. "Sex on the beach for me," Wallace said. "I'll get a banana milkshake," Chiha said. "That will be it," Mel said. "Okay I'll be back with your beverages in a moment." "Man, this place make you have a hard on," Wallace said, after the waitress walked away. "Does this place serve buffalo wings, I'm starving," Nate said. "Yeah, I'm kind of hungry myself," Mel said. Mel looks around for another server. He sees one cleaning off the tables. "Excuse me miss." She comes over to their table. "May I help you?" she asked. "We like an order of buffalo wings," Mel said. "Sure, anything else?" "Yes, may I ask how old are you?" Nate asked. "I'm fourteen." "Fourteen! You're kidding. Your parents let you work in a nude bar?" "Yes, my mother works here too." "Wow!" Nate said. "I'll notify your waiter of your order." She walks away. "Can you guys believe she's only fourteen?" Nate asked. "I kind of knew she was young with that innocent girlish face," Mel said. "But did you see her grapefruits?" Wallace asked. "Grapefruits?" Mel and Nate asked. "Yeah, her tities." "Shut up Wallace. That girl is too young," Mel said. "I can look if I want to. At least she had clothes on." They quickly ate and drank when their waitress brought their drinks and wings. Then they checked in a hotel next to the club. Nate and Chiha have their room. Mel and Wallace have their rooms down the hall. Chiha climbs on the night stand and doses off. Nate was checking out the big screen TV and king size bed. He lays down on the bed and flicks through the channels on the TV. It was nothing interesting but a bunch of pornos on. He turned the TV off then turns over and goes to sleep. While Nate, Chiha, and Wallace were all in their rooms fast asleep, Mel was having a disturbing nightmare. He could see the beast having Sylvia hanging and stabbing her over and over again. He could hear her crying for help. She was dying. Mel woke up from his nightmare. He summoned Wallace and Nate. "Come get up. We must hurry to the dark side." "What happened?" Nate asked. "We must leave at once. Sylvia is in great danger. "We know she's in danger. Those damn creatures have her," Wallace said. "We're sitting around lollygagging and she could already be dead." "Man, I'm tired. We have traveled for several hours," Wallace said. "You listen to me, we are men. No matter what position we are in we strive to win. She's calling for our help. So, let's go rescue our Queen."

Sylvia wakes from her deep sleep. She's lying in a bed with her hands tied together in a dark basement. The door to the basement opens. "Time for you to come upstairs and see the King," the beast said. "Where am I… how did I get here?" Sylvia asked. "No talking!" The beast pulls the rope her hands were tied to, pulling her out of the bed, upstairs. The evil King Lathus was waiting for her. "Sylvia, it's been a long time since we spoke. I hope you've gotten all your beauty sleep." Sylvia was standing in front of him with her head down. "I know you're wondering why I drug you way over here to the dark side." Sylvia kept her head down and kept quiet. "You're a Queen and I'm a King. We're both in the same world but rule separate sides of it. If you join my kingdom, we can rule this whole world together." "I told you before Lathus, I will not be your Queen. You are evil and living evil is not my style. I won't allow you to harm my people." "Why do you wish to be so difficult?" Lathus asked. "I'm not. I'm a Queen that stands up for her people and defines goodness." "Very well then." Lathus stabs Sylvia in the heart with a tranquilizer. She falls to the floor. "Now you and your people will perish," Lathus said, as he leaves the chamber. It was morning when they arrived in the dark side, but it was no sunlight because of the gloominess. "Well here we are," Mel said. Mel parks behind Lathus's place. They were all just sitting there in the ride. "Now how are we going to get in there?" Wallace asked. "We're going to let ourselves in," Mel said. Mel slams down on the gas pedal and the car goes full speed through the door. The car spun in a circle and then stopped. "That's what I call a speedway," Chiha said. They all get out of the car. They're in a lit chamber. It was very quiet. Mel had his hand on his sword just in case they get attacked. "Where could Sylvia be?" Wallace asked. "Hey what about down here?" Nate opened a door that had stairs that led to a basement. Next they heard footsteps and huge shadows appearing. They all became paranoid. The groaning noises seemed to be getting closer and closer. The three beasts appeared. "Trespassers!" one of the beasts yelled. One of the beast, charged Nate and then picked him up. Mel takes his sword and beheads that beast. Nate was back on his feet. The two other beasts were coming after Wallace and Chiha. They were on all four legs, ready for their prey. Chiha crawled on Wallace's shoulder. "What are we going to do? What are we going to do?" Chiha kept asking. Wallace decides to get bold. "Come on you ugly beasts. You want a piece of me." The beasts drew closer, cheesing, ready to eat. Wallace punches one in the mouth. The beast's mouth swelled up. "I knew that would get the smile off your face," he said. Nate comes up behind the other beast and stabs it with his knife. Then Mel beheads it. "I had that one," Nate said. "I know. I like chopping their heads off. Just to make sure they're dead," Mel said. The beast with the swollen mouth, takes off, running. They were all relieved. Still, they had to save Sylvia. They went down to the basement. Sylvia was lying on a bed. They all stood around her. "Sylvia," Mel said. She didn't move. "Sylvia," he whispered in her ear. She still didn't move. Mel tried to feel for a pulse on her neck and her wrist. Nothing. He put his ear to her chest. Still nothing. "Is she… okay?" Nate asked. "No, she's dead," Mel said. "Are you sure? Check her pulse again," Wallace said. Mel puts his ear to her chest and checks her pulse again. "Nope nothing. I'm sorry Sylvia… I let you down," Mel said. He breaks down, crying. So does Wallace. Nate and Chiha feels for them. Mel's tear drops hits Sylvia on the forehead. She begins to glow. They drew away from her. "What's happening?" Nate asked. Sylvia opens her eyes and then she sits up. "Why is everyone looking so sad?" she asked. "We're not sad. We're happy that you're okay," Mel said. They got out of the basement back in the chamber. "Let's get out of here. We have a long journey back home," Mel said. "Yes, you have a long journey back but it's too bad you won't make it back," Lathus said, after he entered the chamber. "Will you gentlemen be so kind to step outside?" Sylvia asked. "Why Sylvia?" Mel asked. "I have a score to settle with the devil." "Let's go," Mel said to the rest of them. They all stepped outside. "Lathus, give me one reason why I shouldn't rip you in half?" "Please, what could you possibly do to me?" "Do you believe in love?" she asked. "What do you think?" "I know you don't. You see, love will always outweigh evil in my heart because I love my people and I love myself. Love conquers. "Quit feeding me this nonsense." Lathus grabs Sylvia's arm but gets shocked. "What the heck?" he said, holding his hand. Sylvia hits him aside his head. Lathus falls to his knees. "You must learn to respect my power of love. You mess with my people you mess with me." "We got your back, Sylvia," Mel said. Sylvia looks back. Mel, Wallace, Nate and Chiha were standing behind her. She smiled. "Let's hurry up and get out of here," Wallace said. Nate opens the passenger side of the car saying, "my Queen." Sylvia takes the passenger seat as the others climb in the back. Mel backs the car out of Lathus's place. Lathus whom, was still left inside, yelled out in anger. His voice started to make the walls shake and the whole place came tumbling down on him. They could hear him from outside screaming until he couldn't be heard anymore. Since Lathus and all the beasts were dead, there was no longer darkness. Nothing but sunshine expanded across the sky. They made their long trip back home.

Everyone in the kingdom were talking and getting worried if Sylvia was going to be brought safely back home. Harper stood before the people. "My fellow friends… Sir Mel and the others have returned." Everyone made noise of joy. The palace doors opened. The people got quiet. Mel, Wallace, and Nate with Chiha on his shoulder, stood at the doors. Harper came to Nate. "Oh, great and noble one… did you bring our Queen back to us?" Mel, Wallace, and Nate turned around and Sylvia was right behind them. The greatest smile came to Harper's face. "The Queen has arrived," Harper said. Everyone jumped for joy. "Oh, my people. I've missed you all," Sylvia said. "Let's hear it for Sir Mel, Wallace, and the great and noble one," Harper said. Everyone shouts, "Hip, hip, hooray!" After Sylvia's return, the day went on. "This is so relaxing after a long day's work," Wallace said to Mel and Nate as they were relaxing in the spa room getting their massages. Even Chiha was getting her little massage on. "Work! You haven't done shit," Mel said. "Look don't start with me." "Well, you don't do anything." "Like you do a whole lot." "I do a lot and plus put in overtime." Here we go again, Nate said to himself. "Why do you always think you're better than everybody else, Mel? Like you're big Willy or something." "Forget I've even said anything to you?" Mel said. Nate turns to Mel when his massage was complete. "I really need to speak to your Queen. Chiha and I need to get home." "I don't see a problem with that now but why don't you want to stay? I don't belong here." "You fit in perfectly. Everyone here looks at you as someone with power. Besides women love a man with power." "Yes, I agree but my world is where I belong." "Come with me," Mel said. "Where are you two going?" Wallace asked.

Sylvia was standing on the balcony outside of her bedroom overlooking the ocean from afar and the sunsetting over it. A knock was at her bedroom door. She opens the door. Harper has his little harp. "You look very lovely this evening my Queen." He bows to her. "Thank you, Harper." "My Queen… may I play a song for you?" "Yes, I would love to hear a song." He begins to play his harp. Sylvia closes her eyes as he plays. The thought of love making crosses her mind, hearing the waves of the ocean and the angelic sounds of the harp. She was really in the groove until one of her guards interrupted them. "Your majesty, the noble one would like to speak to you." "Thank you, Nate said to the guard. The guard salutes him before he left. "Forgive me your majesty for disturbing you, but I really need to speak to you." "Harper, do you mind if I speak with this gentleman, alone?" "No, I do not mind my Queen." He leaves. "What can I do for you Nate?" "Is there any way you can help me get back home?" "Do you know how you got here?" "All I remember was that I was in my spacecraft. I hit a meteor and for some unusual reason, I ended up here. My spacecraft is totally destroyed." Chiha appeared out of nowhere. She ran up Nate's leg and sat on his shoulder. "This a cute monkey," she said, rubbing on Chiha. Chiha made a funny face at her. "So, can you help me?" Nate asked, again. "Oh, I'm sorry Nate. I'm just a Queen that rule a world. I'm not a magician or a wizard that can perform magic, but I wish I could, but I can't." Sylvia starts walks away. "May I ask you a question, a personal question?" Nate asked. Sylvia turns around. "How come a woman like you is ruling over an entire world all by yourself?" "What do you mean by a woman like me?" "I mean, I'm not trying to sound sexist or anything. I just thought whenever there's a Queen, there's always a King." "Yes, you're right. I had a husband, but he passed away recently." "I'm sorry to hear that. How did he die?" "He had a bad heart." "He was an old man?" Nate asked. "Yes, he was very old. Alijal and I were honest to each other about everything. I guess his heart was the only thing he kept secret. Do you have someone special in your life?" she asked. "I did. I use to have a wife, but we're not together no more because she decided to have a child with someone else." "That's too bad. Good people seem to always lose the one they truly love," Sylvia said, "but I keep my husband with me in my heart. Can I show you something, Nate?" "Sure," he said. They took a long walk through her home to a door on the other side of the palace. "Behind this door, is my little secret." Sylvia opens the door. It's a place with a bed of roses and above an opening for the moonlight to shine down upon the garden and the sunshine to shine on the garden in the day. "This is amazing. I haven't seen nothing like this," Nate said. "This is my sacred garden. It's the one place I come to be to myself or when I'm hurting to ease the pain." Nate and Chiha hear music. "Do you hear that?" Sylvia asked. Sylvia points to the sky. Above were singing angels gliding through the air. They stood in the middle of the garden just listening to the beautiful music. Sylvia had her eyes closed as tears streamed down her face. Then she put both her hands over her face. She cried even more. "Sylvia, what's wrong?" Nate asked. "Oh, Nate, I'm tired of being alone. I miss him so much." She buried her face in his chest. "Sylvia, Sylvia look at me." She looked at him. "Will you stay here with me? I can't rule this world and be in this big place by myself." "What do you mean you can't? You've been doing it. You got all these strong men to protect you. A whole lot of people who love you and look up to you. I even look up to you. I think a woman who rules and takes a stand for her people is appealing to me. I like independent women. So, you don't need me. All you need is someone who will always have back. Your people have your back. And your husband... that's why he never told you about his heart. He didn't want you to worry. He knew you was strong enough to stand on your own. So, don't be afraid Sylvia. You are not alone."

Nate and Chiha take a long walk to the beach that night. Nate sits down on the sand. So does Chiha. He stares at the pretty moon in the sky. "Well Chiha… I guess we're stuck here. "Don't say that. This could all be a dream," Chiha said. "I doubt it. My family probably thinks I've been kidnapped or laying somewhere dead now." "I still think this is all a dream." "We'll see when I wake up in the morning." Nate lays back and slowly drifts off to sleep.

Sylvia was standing on her balcony, gazing at the sky. A sea gull perches itself on the ledge. "Well, hello Mr. Gull," Sylvia said. "Good evening, Sylvia. How is your evening going?" Mr. Gull asked. "Oh, it's been breathtaking." "Sylvia, your knight in shining armour seems to be very homesick." "Yes, maybe there is something I could do. I hate to see him unhappy." "Goodnight Sylvia." "Thank you for your time Mr. Gull." The sea gull flies away. Sylvia goes back inside, turns off her light, and gets into bed. She closes her eyes but quickly opens them. Sylvia sits up in her bed staring at the opened balcony door, waiting for someone to come through it. Nothing happens. She knows now, she's the only ruler in this world. No more darkness, only sunshine.

Nate and Chiha wakes up in the morning, still on the beach. "See I told you this wasn't no dream," Nate said. "Face it, Nate. This has to be our fate. Maybe it was meant for us to be here." "So, what are you saying? We died and went to heaven? Wait! That could be it." Nate stood up and headed back to Sylvia's place. "Wait for me," Chiha said. Mel and the guards were out front. "Nate, I've been looking all over for you. I hope you're not upset at us," Mel said. "No. It's nobody's fault I ended up here." "We really want you to stay here, Nate but we really want you to be happy." They had something huge covered up with a huge sheet. Mel and the guards uncovered it. Nate's spacecraft was rebuilt and restored. "How did you guys rebuild it and so quick?" Nate asked. "All the men here pitched in," Mel said. Sylvia and many people in the kingdom, gathered around. "How can I ever thank you?" Nate asked. "It's nothing," Mel said. "You people are something. I have a whole lot of love for you guys." "We all love you too Nate," Sylvia said. "Are you sure you don't want to stay, great one?" Harper asked. "I'm sure but I'll miss you guys." Everyone waves goodbye as Nate and Chiha board the spacecraft. "Thank you, Nate. Thank you for help rescuing me and showing me," Sylvia said. He gave her a thumbs up. "Boy, I'm ready to get back home. Are you ready Nate," Chiha asked. Nate looks at Mel, Wallace, and Sylvia through the window of his spacecraft. "Not quite," he said. Nate gets out of the spacecraft. Nate looks at Mel. "Mel, you know you're the man." "Take care," Mel said. They give each other a hug. Then he turns to

Wallace. Wallace was rubbing his eyes. "You okay Wallace?" Nate asked. "Yeah," he answered, turning away. "Are you crying?" Mel asked. "I not crying!" he shouted. "I just got some sand in my eyes." Nate gave Wallace a hug. "It's okay to show how you feel." Sylvia was looking at the ground when Nate looked at her. "You know I'll miss you the most," he said with his hand under her chin so she would look up. Always keep your head up, no matter what. Can you do that for me?" Sylvia nodded her head. "I'll be thinking about you," she said. "I'll be thinking about you," Nate said. He kissed her on the cheek and hugged her. Then she places her head against his chest. "I know you have a lot of love in you Nate. I can tell by the strong beat of your heart." Sylvia, should a Queen wear her crown?" Harper asked, holding a pillow with a crown sitting on it. It was made of diamonds. Sylvia places the crown on her head. It was her time now. Time for her to rise.

IN ALL THESE YEARS

Sylvia opened her eyes to a bright and early morning, knowing it was going to be another beautiful day. She hopped out of bed to get on her gigantic built-in wall computer. It was the last day of January 2012 and the past thirty days have been wonderful. Sylvia is really looking forward to February because her best friend, Magalina was getting married in two weeks. Wallace delivered her the invitation two days ago. Sylvia had chuckled at the fact that she and her fiancé, Strew, were getting married when she first got the invitation because strew, is over six feet tall. Magalina is only four feet tall. Just think how their children will come out to be, she thought. Before Sylvia heard about the wedding, the memory of Nate, the man from the planet Earth came in her mind a lot recently. She couldn't get him out of her mind ever since he went away. As time went by, she knew she had to forget about him. There was a time when she thought he wasn't real. He was just a man in her imagination. Because Mel had somewhat befriended him, never spoke about him in all these years. It's ten years since then. But then Sylvia would say to herself, he had to be real. He was here with Mel and Wallace when they rescued me from the dark side. He was brave. He didn't know what he was getting himself into when he got here. Two weeks finally came. The wedding was held in a memorial hall where all the Kings and Queens and many other people married. This day was as exciting as watching the Royal Wedding on TV. The color Magalina chose was cream color. Like they say nobody's supposed to look better than the bride but by Sylvia being the maid of honor and best friend, Magalina suggested she look as good as she. The ceremony went quick. Soon as they jumped the broom, everyone headed to this erotic club for the reception. All the children had to stay behind and be looked after by nannies. Magalina and Strew were an inseparable couple. They did everything together. Like most couples, before they get married, the men have a bachelor party, the women have a bridal shower and bachelorette party, but they have their parties together. Strew danced with female strippers, Magalina danced with male strippers, and so did everyone else. Sylvia didn't. She just wanted to sit back, drink champagne and watch everyone have a good time. Wallace danced with as many women as he could. Mel came over to Sylvia. "You not going to dance?" "Naah, I'm fine, right here with my champagne." Mel went back to partying. Sylvia drank quite a bit of champagne, she became tipsy. One of the male dancers asked her to dance. This time she was willing but could barely stand. They danced close. Sylvia still had her drink in her hand. She liked having his muscular half-naked body against hers. "Do you know how long it's been since I've been in a man's arms?" He didn't answer her. He just kept on grinding on her. She started hiccupping, then took a sip of her champagne. After everyone was partied out, it was time to chow. When everyone was done eating, a couple of the cocktail servers wheeled out a seven- layer wedding cake. It was white with coconut flakes and pineapples. Everybody applauded. The happily married couple stood by the cake to get their picture taken. Everyone took another picture on their cell phones of Strew cutting the cake. Then someone decides to invade on the party.

"I can't believe someone's having a party and I wasn't invited," Veel, who was Lathus's widow. Sylvia could not stand the sight of her nor could anyone else. She had long jet- black hair and horrifying make-up. Looking at her was like depression. Lathus made her leave their kingdom many, many years ago because she wanted to have power over him instead of just being a wife. That's why Lathus tried to get Sylvia to be with him. Sylvia knows this world isn't big enough for the both of them. "Nobody don't want you here," someone said. "I can't believe that. I'm a part of this extraordinary place too." "You're a witch and witches aren't invited to weddings." "Oh, is that so," Veel said. She walked over to the wedding cake and scooped up some icing with her finger and tasted it. "This is some good cake." "What do you want Veel?" Sylvia asked. "To be honest I was out and about looking for a new King." Wallace started laughing. "Who in the world would want to marry her? Let alone fuck her," he said in a tone he thought she wouldn't hear him. Veel heard what he said. "That's funny coming from you with all the girls you've got caught up with… what's their names… Gonorrhea, Chlamydia, Syphilis, and HIV… I hear she's a real killer." Wallace's face turned red in embarrassment. "Now like I was saying, I'm looking for a King. I want to create new generation so we can have more Kings and Queens." "You don't want to cooperate with anyone so how you're going to manage that?" Sylvia asked. "I'm the most cooperative and loving person there is." "The many years I've known you, I don't think so." "Oh, you go to hell Sylvia. You think you're so much better than anyone else. When I find me a King you ain't going to be shit. That palace of yours is going to be destroyed and you're going to be scrubbing my floors and making my bed every day when I'm done with you." "Dream on," Sylvia said. "I'm going to be your nightmare." Veel ran out. Everybody at the reception continued on with the party as if she never showed up. When the reception was over, Sylvia and Mel just realized Wallace had already left. They headed back to the palace. Mel knocked on his door. Wallace opened his door. "What is it?" "We want to talk to you," Sylvia said. "About what?" "You mind if we come in?" He let them in his room. "Is there something going on with you that you want to talk about?" "You're asking because of what that evil lady said?" "Well, is true that you caught those diseases?" she asked. Wallace turned away and said, "no, it's not." "Are you sure?" "Look

I told you no so will you please go away." "Wallace we just want to help you." "Yeah, we don't want to find out one day you're dying of AIDS or something," Mel said. "You're the one with AIDS because you're the one that's a homosexual!" "I've had it with you!" Mel walked out. Sylvia left out behind him. She caught up with Mel. "I can care less about him," Mel said, "he can catch on fire and burn for all I care." "It's okay, he's the one suffering… I just know it," she said.

All the people in Sedonia gathered on the shore at sunset to have a candlelight vigil on a day called the "Day of Remembrance." Everyone kept quiet to reminiscence of all the love ones that went away. Afterwards, Sylvia went to her sacred garden to pray about her late husband, Alijal. The angels sung a song. She slept peacefully that night.

The next day, in the early afternoon, Sylvia was coming down the hallway when Harper had grabbed her by the arm saying," you must come with me my Queen." "Where are we going?" "To the throne room… he is coming." "He who?" Sylvia asked. Harper just kept pulling her along. They got to the throne room and a lot of people were standing around. "Excuse me, pardon me," Harper said, as he and Sylvia passed through the crowd. "Wait here," he said. Harper opened one of the palace doors and Mel came up to him and whispered, "he's coming." Harper smiled a great smile and shouted over and over again, "he's coming!" Sylvia and the people didn't know what he was talking about, but Harper kept running in circles. The guards outside had opened up the doors and they seen a silhouette of a man coming. Sylvia's eyes got big. "It can't be—Alijal! Could he really have come back from the dead?" This was a silhouette of a younger man. When she finally seen who the man was, she still couldn't believe it. "This is like déjà vu except everyone knows me now," Nate said. "I can't believe you're here," Sylvia said. "Well, I'm here so how are you my Queen?" "Seeing you, I'm better." She gazed at him. "You look so different now." "Yeah, I have gotten older." "But you still look wonderful," Sylvia said. "You still look bold and beautiful, "Nate said. Harper walked up to them and said, "maybe you two should be alone." "If that's what the Queen wants," Nate said. Wallace comes around asking, "What's going on around here?" "Hey, Wally how you been?" Nate tries to give him a handshake. "You again. How long you going to be stuck here this time American man? And my name isn't no damn Wally, get it!" Wallace walks away. "I can see some people haven't changed," Nate said. "He has issues. Come on I want us to go talk somewhere alone," Sylvia said. They went outside of the palace and took a walk. "I can't believe it's been ten years… it's seems like yesterday," she said. "In those years I've been eager to come back here," he said. "I didn't think it would be okay at first." "Why did you think that?" "I thought found another or got married again but since I've stayed in touch with Mel, he tells me how everything is going with you, him and everybody. Not that I'm trying to keep tabs on you or anything." "Oh, I didn't know that," Sylvia said. "I've had my share of relationships, but they never lasted because none of them measured up to you. I missed you, Sylvia. I've been yearning to see your pretty face again." "I missed you too." They continued to walk, and they held hands. "Where's your little monkey?" "Chiha is back in Australia. I couldn't no longer keep her." "What really made you come back after all this time?" "It was time plus this is like a vacation and I needed it." "How long you gonna stay?" "For a while. I plan on spending all the time I have with you." The hand of hers he was holding, he kissed it as they walked along.

Wallace was walking around in his room, frustrated. I don't know he's doing here but this is all I need is someone other than Mel telling me how to be a gentleman, respect the ladies and I know Sylvia gonna tell him to talk to me. I'm about to stand around here and wait for them to approach me with more of their talk. A getaway is going to do me some good. He leaves the palace without being noticed.

Sylvia takes Nate for a ride on her white stallion on the beach. They rode for an hour. Then they stopped to walk on the beach. "He's always been here for me, haven't you boy," she said, patting her horse. Her stallion neighed. "Now I'm here." Nate pulls her close. "Are you hungry? I have great chefs that can cook us a great meal." "Sure," he said, "I have a question… since I'll be staying in this beautiful home of yours for a while, where will I be sleeping?" "In a guest room." "In a guest room," he replied. "Yeah, where did you think you'd be sleeping? Let's take him back to the stables." They went to the kitchen after they came in the palace. "Wow, this kitchen is big," Nate said. The kitchen smelled of barbecue, boiled potatoes, and cakes being baked. "This is Amu the top chef and this is Lunia my other chef." "Hello," they both said. They both were cutting vegetables. "Hello. Whatever you guys are cooking sure smells good." "I love these guys," Sylvia said. "Let me show you the dining room." "Lovely," he said when he seen it. A long table with a lace table cloth, glass plates, spoons, knives and forks laid properly. Tall candles placed in crystal candle holders. A chandelier hangs above. "You eat like this every day?" "Yeah." "Must be nice. You ever cook for yourself?" he asked. "Yeah, every now and then. If it's late in the evening and I'm hungry I like to fix myself something. Now let's go wash up for dinner." After they got their bellies full, Sylvia took Nate down to the spa room. He recognized the women from the last time. "Ladies, this man needs to be took care of." "Well the noble one has returned," one of the women said. "So, would you still like that massage?" Sylvia looked at Nate with a smile and said, "Give him the works." "As you wish my Queen." "Have fun," Sylvia said to Nate when she was leaving the spa. "I guess I'll go in the back and get undressed," he said. "Oh, no noble one, you don't have to do anything. We do all the work." One of them helped him out of his uniform. "Nice underwear," another woman said. She walked behind him and pulled back his underwear to see what kind they were. "Hanes," she said, "nice." Then she pulled them down. His underwear were down at his ankles now. "Step out of them please." He stepped out of them. "Come this way." They lead him to the shower. Man, these women are aggressive, Nate thought to himself. All four of the women surrounded him. They began thoroughly cleansing him. One did his back and backside, one did his arms and arm pits, one did his chest and down low and the other one did his legs and feet. Nate couldn't believe it. He was living every man's fantasy. Him taking a shower with four partially nude women. If he told all his friends back home, they would be jealous, or they probably wouldn't believe him. Nate puts on a robe after the massage. He runs into Mel while going down the hall to find Sylvia. "You're squeaky clean. Just coming from the spa, huh?" "Yes." "The spa treatment is my favorite thing too. It's great to be pampered like that. Every guy here gets it except for Wallace." "What's up with him? Has he always been idiotic?" Nate asked. "As long as I've known him, yeah. He's been worse lately because he's going through some things, but I don't give a fuck though. He thinks his dick is seven inches longer than every man in the universe and wants to screw everything with two legs that's why he's going through. Well, I've got to get going and I know you want to catch up with the Queen. She's probably in her room, you can keep going down this hallway. See you around." Mel gives him a salute. Nate salutes him back. Sylvia was lying on her bed with her eyes closed while Harper plays his harp for her. Nate stood in the doorway, loving the sounds of the harp. Sylvia opened her eyes and saw Nate in the doorway. "All done?" she asked. Harper stopped playing. "Don't mind me I was enjoying the music," Nate said. "I think that's enough for tonight," Sylvia said, "Thanks Harper." "No problem my Queen. Have a good evening and to you noble one." She gets up after Harper left and Nate goes to her. "So, what do you have planned now?" "Let's take a walk through my home."

Wallace was sitting in a topless bar, drunk. He went to about every club in Sedonia drinking the night away. Going back to the palace was somewhere he wasn't about to go at the moment. Besides he was too drunk to drive himself anywhere. A motel was where he had plans of staying for the night. He was kind of dizzy when he tried to stand up. Someone sat next to him. "You're really messed up," the person said. He didn't know who it was at first until he was able to see straight. That horrifying face. How could he have not known. "You… what do you want?" he asked Veel. She lights a cigarette. "What are you still cruising around for a King?" She takes a puff and blows out. Then Veel leans back, put both elbows on the bar and crosses her legs so the split in her dress can show off her thighs. Wallace turns his head. "Maybe," she finally says. "You're in the wrong place." He wasn't looking at her. "Maybe you can help me." "Why would I want to help you? You're poison and I don't mess with poison." "You could have fooled me," Veel said. "You're in the one place where you pick up all these whores and then face the consequences because you don't take responsibility for your actions. I even know how many times you've been to the clinic." "For your information I'm just down here because I'm just trying to avoid Sylvia, her boyfriend, and everybody." "Sylvia has a boyfriend now?" "Yeah, she met him many years ago. He's from someplace called Earth." "Really. I would like to see what this boyfriend from Earth is like." "You can't do that." "Oh, yes, I am. If you try to stop me, I'll tell Sylvia you have AIDS and I have the power to make your body deteriorate so you'll look like you're dying of it." Wallace was tempted to run but he knew she was for real. He shouldn't of opened his big mouth. "Whatever you want," he said. "That's a good boy. This is what we're going to do…"

Sylvia takes Nate to his room after their long tour. "What's this?" Nate asked. "One of the guest rooms. This is where you're going to sleep for the rest of your stay." "I'm not ready to go to sleep. Why don't we go to your room? It's things we can do." "Like what?" she asked. "You know." "We both need to get some sleep Nate. We have lots to do tomorrow." "Okay whatever you say." "I'll have one of my housekeepers to bring you an extra blanket in case you get cold, goodnight." "Goodnight? Don't I get a kiss?" he asked. Sylvia shook her head and answered, "no." She walked away after that. "Oh, I see she wants to play hard to get. I guess I'll have to play along." Soon as Wallace got up in the morning in his motel, he showered and rinsed his mouth out with Scope. He hurried up and got dressed before Veel showed up. "I thought you were going to be in disguise?" he asked her. "Of course." With her powers she transformed herself into a younger pretty woman with long ravishing red hair, smooth skin and with a simple but catchy dress on. "Let's go see the Queen," she said in her innocent sounding voice. Sylvia knocks on Nate's bedroom door but then let's herself in. "Rise and shine." Nate was still knocked out, laying on the other end of the bed. Sylvia stood over him and yelled, "Nate!" in his ear. He woke up and almost fell out of bed. "Time to get dressed hun." "What time is it?" he asked. "After nine o' clock. I hope you had enough sleep; we have a long day ahead of us." "What are we doing?" "First, we're going to my friend Magalina's house. Her and her husband wants us to have brunch with them." "What's the next thing?" "Shopping! So, hurry and get washed up I have a tailor that will have you fit in with everyone here." "As long as I'm still looking like a stud." "Don't worry. You'll still look like the stud muffin you are." Nate got groomed and fitted then looked himself over in the mirror. "I don't look half bad." Sylvia had left but came back and said, "Wow what a transformation." He turned and looked at her. "You look lovely as always." "Thanks, you look like the stud you always have been. Let's get our day started." Wallace and Veel arrived at Sylvia's thirty minutes after she and Nate had left. Mel acknowledged them after the guards let them in. "Is Sylvia around?" Wallace asked. "No, she just left," Mel asked. "I wanted her to meet Licia. You know when she's going to come back?" "Not until this evening." "We'll just come back later," Wallace said to Licia. "Wallace, can we talk?" Mel asked. "Yeah, go ahead." "Privately." "Ok." "Excuse us," Mel said to Licia. They went down an empty hallway. "Who's the lady?" "A friend." "What is her business it with Sylvia?" "We can only discuss it with Sylvia." "Any stranger that enters the Queen's home when she's not present, I should know about it even if it's just to discuss something." "Well tough I'm not telling you anything." Wallace to get Licia so they can leave. "You hold it right there!" Mel said. "Let's get out of here," Wallace said. "Wait let me handle him," Licia said. "Excuse me sir I only wanted to see the Queen about a job. You see I'm tired of doing what I'm doing now and I'm just ready to make a change." "What do you do?" Mel asked. "Right now?" she asked. He nodded. "I'm a dancer—an exotic dancer. Would you like to see what I can do? She started playing with his braids. "I can strip for you." She untied the front of her dress so he could see her breasts. "I don't want to see that. Come back tomorrow or something when Sylvia is here." "Gladly," Licia said. They left. "He must be gay," she said. "Tell me about it," Wallace said. "What do we do now? Sylvia's not going to be back for a while." "We'll be back, for sure," Licia said.

Sylvia, Nate, Magalina, and Strew sat outside on an elegant patio of a cafe where they could enjoy the early afternoon. Sylvia told Magalina and Strew how she and Nate met and where he was from. Nate told them how different Earth was from Sedonia. They were fascinated by his story. Then they all went shopping nearby at some outdoor shops and they went to nearly every store. The last stop they made was at a perfume store. Nate and Strew decided to wait outside while the ladies looked in that store. "I've never been happier in my life," Magalina said, trying on different perfumes. "I know, it shows," Sylvia said. "It's great being in love." "Are you saying you and Nate are in love?" "Possibly." Meanwhile, outside of the perfume shop, Nate said, "I think I love her." "You think?" Strew asked. "Yeah, she doesn't compare to any woman I ever met." "If she's the one for you, you shouldn't have a doubt. But I wonder how are you two going to maintain a relationship? Are you planning on staying here?" "That's good question. I do have something to ask her." Creeping around nearby was Veel still disguised as Licia. She used her special powers to find out where Sylvia was. She saw Sylvia come out of the shop and hug Nate. "So, that must be the boyfriend. Yes, he is fit for a King and she's going to be out of luck."

Veel returned to her place near the dark side and where she kept Wallace prisoner. Her own little domain she lived in since she departed from Lathus. Now she thinks it's her time to be the ruler of Sedonia. She changed back into her original self. "I have found my King," she said to Wallace. "Veel this is really not a good idea." "Shut up. I am going to take over Sedonia and I know just how to do it. For many years I've watched Sylvia reign over Sedonia, now her time has passed. With me being the Queen and my King by my side, we'll rule a great kingdom." "I'm trying to tell you he is in love with Sylvia." "That's all about to change when he hears the truth about her. Now it's time to cast my spell." She woke ten beasts from the dark side from the dead. Wallace was stiff with fear when the beasts appeared. Their bloody red eyes and their huge furry bodies made them scarier than her. "Welcome my pets. We have a job to do." "Hey what about me?" Wallace asked. "You're staying here." "You can't keep me in this hell hole forever." Veel kept him prisoner as she and the beasts head to Sylvia's palace. Sylvia and Nate got back to the palace as soon as night came, and Mel wanted to tell her about the woman Wallace brought by, but he didn't. Nate went straight to his room to change. Then Sylvia came to his room. "You not tired, are you?" "No, not at all." "Let's go for a ride on the beach," she said. They rode around for a while then Nate wanted to stop. They got off the horse and sat in the sand. "I like you a lot Sylvia. I've been having a great time. I would love it if you came to Earth with me." "Really... your world!" "Yes." "I don't know. I can't be away from my home too long." "Just for a couple of days," Nate said. "But will the people there like me because I remember you telling me how the people there can be." "You're only get to meet my family and my friends so you're only around the people I love, and they'll love you." "Of course, I'll go with you." She gives him a hug. Then they kissed. Then Nate lays her down in the sand and they kissed again. He starts pulling up her dress and felt underneath. He didn't feel anything. No panties, he thought. "No Nate." "What's wrong?" he asked. "You don't like having sex on the beach?" She got up. "I want to go get wet." Sylvia ran into the water. She soaked her whole body and came back out. "That felt good." He could see everything through her dress. "Let's get back home," Sylvia said. They got back on the stallion and rode back. Definitely no panties, he thought again. She was nearly dried off when she got home. Nate pulled her damp dress over her head when they were in her bedroom. As she stood naked before him, she said, "we have to use a condom." "You don't trust me?" he asked. "No, it's just--- it's been a long time. "It's been a long time since we've seen each other." "You have one?" Nate asked. "Yes." After they made love, they laid in bed caressing each other. "It has been a long time," he said, looking at her. Veel had arrived. One of the guards at the door pointed his spear and said, "holt!" Veel cast her spell of sleeping gas. The two guards fell asleep. She and the beasts entered the place. Mel and some of the other guards dropped off to sleep because of the sleeping gas spell she cast upon them. "I'm going to catch up with Mel," Nate said, getting dressed. "Get your rest we are leaving tomorrow. He kissed Sylvia on the forehead. When Nate went down the hall, Veel and the beasts were waiting there. "Well hello handsome. Would you like to come with me?" "What?" Nate said. One of the beasts shot him with a tranquilizer. He fell to the floor. "I thought you'd agree with me," she said. "Let's go we got what we came for." Two of the beasts picked him up and carried him. An hour has passed. Sylvia woke up and saw that Nate wasn't by her side. She put on her robe and went looking for him in the palace. Who she found in the throne room was Mel and some of the guards waking up off the floor. "What's going on?" she asked. "Veel… she was here," Mel said. Sylvia's eyes got wide. "She put us to sleep." "Oh no, have you seen Nate?" "No, the last I've seen him he was with you." "Where could he be?" Sylvia asked.

Wallace was determined to escape. He searched the place for something to help him escape. He found an ax on the wall and he got a hold of it. With all his might, he axed the giant wooden door. Now that he known he was free, Wallace dropped the ax and made his escape. "Got to get to the palace." He knows he's probably too late.

Sylvia and Mel looked around the whole palace but couldn't find Nate. "I'm going to get changed and we're going to look on the beach for him," she said to Mel. "Right," he said. Sylvia hurries to her bedroom to put on some comfortable clothes. Then her computer came on. Veel was on the screen. "Hello Sylvia. I know what you're looking for and I have him." "What have you've done with Nate?" "Don't worry he's alright but he's going to be perfect when he becomes my King and I'm his Queen. Your days of being Queen are numbered Sylvia." "You'll never be Queen." "Who's going to stop me? You? Come and try." The screen went blank. "This means war," Sylvia said clutching her fists. "You're really taking the search for Nate seriously," Mel said after she got dressed and was ready. Sylvia was dressed like she was ready to fight a battle with a sword at her side. "Veel kidnapped Nate. Get all the guards--- it's time for war!" "Sylvia!" Wallace came rushing in, happy to see her. "Where's Nate?" he asked. "Where have you been?" Sylvia asked. "It's a long story." "Nate's been taken. We're going to get him back." "Let me come too." "No, you stay here. I'm taking Mel and the guards with me. Let's get moving," she said.

Nate just woke up from his long nap. He was unsure where he was at. All he knew was in a bedroom, his hands and feet were chained down to the bed. He was stripped down to nothing but his boxers on. A door opens.

Veel comes in and stands at the foot of the bed. "Who are you? Why am I here? Why am I in these chains?" "You have nothing to worry about. I'm here to help you." "Why did you shoot me with a tranquilizer?" "I had to. I didn't know if you were going to do something to me." "Do something to you?" Nate said. "I don't know what you're talking about." "I've been watching you with Sylvia. I think you're making a big mistake getting involved with her." "Lady, what are you talking about?" "Sylvia hasn't had a man in her life in forever. So, by her being a Queen, she thinks she runs everybody, especially men. She'll have you dressing the way she wants you to dress, go only to places she wants to go… that's why she lost the husband she had." "She told me he died of a heart attack," Nate said. "That's what she wants you to believe." Veel moves closer to him, running her hand up his leg. "Me, on the other hand, knows how to stand behind her man. Don't you think it's better being King and having a Queen that will be by your side. Not the kind that wants to tell you how to be." "You think I'm supposed to fall for you? I don't even know you." "Wouldn't you like to find out?" "Look I know Sylvia is a great person. I see it in the eyes of the people. She has so much love and loyalty. Her people would do anything for her. "I am more woman than she'll ever be." "If you're so much better than Sylvia, how come you don't have a husband?" "I just don't." "You can't get one because you're too busy running around here with those ugly ass creatures that look worse than you." "How dare you!" Veel made a ball of fire appear in her hand. "Have you ever heard of the burning bed?" she asked. "Hey, what are you trying to do?" "You better apologize to me or I'll barbecue your ass!" "Okay, I'm sorry. I didn't mean to call you ugly." Veel made her little ball of fire disappear then shot him in the neck with a tranquilizer. Nate went back into a deep sleep. "You're not royalty material anyway. You're gonna die and so is Sylvia. I know she's coming and she's going to regret coming here." Sylvia and her troops arrived at Veel's secluded domain in no time. They entered through the opened front door. "Veel!... Nate!" Sylvia called. No one answered. It seemed like no one was there. Then Veel appears out of nowhere. "Sylvia it's so nice to see you but too bad I have to run." She disappeared then reappeared in the front doorway. "You guys are probably cold. I'm going to heat it up for you." She disappeared again. "Why does she keep disappearing?" Mel asked. "Forget about her. We need to find Nate," Sylvia said. They split up. It was two hidden rooms. Sylvia and some of the guards looked in one of the rooms. The one Mel and the other guards looked in; Nate was in that room. He was still chained down on the bed, unconscious. "Sylvia!" Mel called. She came running. "Oh, Nate what happened to you?" she embraced him. "Let's get him out of these chains." "What's that smell?" one of the guards asked. "It smells like something's burning," another guard said. "Let's get out of here," Sylvia said. Nate was carried shoulder to shoulder by Mel and one of the guards. They couldn't get out the front entry because it was on fire and the fire was spreading. They looked for another way out. There was a back door, but it was pad locked. Mel zapped it with his lazer gun. They all got out quick because everyone was choking from the smoke. The roof of the building had collapsed. They got into their rides and headed back to the palace.

Wallace was worried about Sylvia and even about Mel. This whole situation was fault. He felt so guilty for how he's been over the years. If somebody dies, he'll never be able to live with himself. Then Veel came marching into the palace with all the beasts. "You stay away from me!" Wallace said. "Nothing to fear because it's my time to reign now. Veel commanded all the beasts to bring all the people in Sedonia they could get from their homes to the palace. "What do you think you're doing?" he asked Veel. The beasts left. "You'll will see shortly." Since they were in the throne room, Veel took a seat in Sylvia's chair. He stared at her as she sat there comfortably in the Queen's chair and he said, "oh my God."

The beasts have taken every woman, man, and child from their homes and brought them all to the palace. Magalina and Strew couldn't understand why they were being brought in by these beasts into Sylvia's home in the middle of the night. But everyone became wide-eyed when they saw Veel. "Hey, it's that witch again!" the same man from the wedding reception said. "Silence! Or I'll have you hung," Veel said. "What's the meaning of this? Where's Sylvia?" someone asked. All the people began talking all at once. "The Queen you once knew has perished," she said. When Wallace heard that, his heart melted. "I'm the Queen now, so everybody is going to bow down to me!" The man came forward. "Nobody's going to bow down to an evil thing like you," he said, shaking his fist in the air. "So, you're not going to bow to me?" "Hell no!" Veel nodded at one of the beasts. Two of the beasts grabbed the man. "Get your hands off me!" They laid him on a table with his head hanging off the edge. One held him down when the other beast beheaded the man with an ax. All the people backed away as his head rolled through the crowd, then stopped when it hit the wall. Everyone was rattled with fear. "Now everybody, get on your knees and bow to me or the same thing is going to happen to someone else!" Everyone got on their knees and bowed. Magalina was the only one that wouldn't. "Did you hear what I said?" Magalina just glared at Veel. "Get on your knees and bow to me." "No!" Magalina yelled. "Maggie what are you doing?" Strew asked, raising from his knees. Veel came closer and screamed," get on your knees you damn dwarf!" "No!" she yelled louder. "Go burn in hell bitch!" "Get rid of her," Veel said to the beasts. One of the beasts went to grab her and Magalina slapped the beast. Then two of them grabbed them grabbed her. "Get your filthy paws off me!" They pushed the headless body off the table then laid

Magalina on her stomach. "No! No!" Strew yelled when he saw them raising the ax. He laid on her and then looked up at the beasts saying, "please don't kill my wife, please!" "Put the ax down," Veel said. The beast put the ax down. "You'd better tell that wife of yours to mind me and get on her knees." "Honey listen to me… let's just do what she says. It will be okay." She listens to her husband. They get on their knees and bowed. "I'm the Queen of this world and no one's going to stop me!" The palace doors flew open. "No, I am the Queen of Sedonia!" Sylvia and her guards stood in the doorway ready for a fight. Wallace stood up when he heard Sylvia's voice. He praised the Lord. "Don't you ever die?" Veel asked. "No, but you are," Sylvia said. "I would like everyone to leave the room. Including you, Mel." "Why Sylvia? You shouldn't be left alone with her," Mel said. "Don't worry, I got this. Keep an eye on Nate for me. He'll be waking up soon." Everybody went in the dining room. Mel, Wallace and with Nate, and the guards all went outside. The beasts stood around being quiet. Veel snatched the ax from one of the beasts. "I'm gonna cut you into pieces and scatter you all over Sedonia." Sylvia pulled out her sword. "We'll see about that." Veel raised the ax, then swung it at her. She kept missing because Sylvia kept moving. Sylvia backed up, but ended up tripping on her own feet so Veel cut her in the side. Sylvia was sitting on the floor with her hand on her wound. "Well, well, well… looks like this is it for you." She raised the ax. "This won't hurt—much." As the ax was coming down upon her, Sylvia quickly picked up her sword and cut off half of Veel's arm. Veel screamed when she saw half her arm on the floor with the ax still in the hand. She was getting woozy from losing a lot of blood. She fell down and started whining. Sylvia stood up and said, "didn't see that coming, did you?" Mel and the others came in to see what was going on. All the people came back too. Sylvia turned towards everybody. "I don't want to die," Veel said, looking like she was going to pass out. Sylvia ignored her. "Who are you to turn your back on me and leave me to die?" "Oh, I recall you leaving me and my men to die." "I hope you die soon and fall in a pit of fire," Veel said, "or better yet I hope you die of an illness or…" With a quick swing of her sword, Sylvia beheaded Veel. "Why don't you just die?" Since Veel was dead, her spell had lifted, and all the beasts vanished. Everyone stood quietly. Then everyone chanted, "Long lives the Queen! Long lives the Queen!" Sylvia walks towards Mel and Nate. She blacks out and falls. Mel catches her.

Sylvia stayed in bed that day after the doctor treated her wound. A nurse stayed with her while she remained in her room. She was feeling lonely without her friends around, so Sylvia asked for them. Magalina and Strew came first. Magalina hugged her and kissed her on the forehead. "I heard how brave you were," Sylvia said. "She's my little firecracker," Strew said, "even though she scared me half to death." After they left, Mel and Wallace came in next. "You look marvelous my Queen. I know you'll get better soon," Mel said. "Of course. I'm down but not for long." Wallace was ready to say something but was nervous. "I have a confession to make... I... it was my fault for what all has happened." "Veel was Veel. She would of tried something on her own, regardless if she had help or not," she said. "Another thing... would you forgive me for being such an egotistical bastard for all these years?" She touched him on the face. "Of course, I'll forgive you. I've always cared about you Wallace. Just be yourself. You don't have to prove anything. People will like you and respect you for that." He laid his head in her lap and cried. After they left, Nate came in. "My love," he said. He sat down next to her, holding her hand. "You're my hero, you know that? You're always risking your life for everybody. "You've done the same for me," Sylvia said. "Sorry I can't go to your world with you." "Don't worry about that. I'm staying here until you heal."

Fireworks lit up the sky of that evening. All the people of Sedonia gathered outside of the palace. Sylvia appeared in a diamond gown with a diamond crown on her head. Nate stood by her side and everyone continued to watch the fireworks. Sylvia was proud to know she finally declared her independence.

JOURNEY TO THIS PLACE CALLED EARTH

It was a new and beautiful day in Sedonia. Queen Sylvia sits on the throne and awaits what Wallace was coming to tell her. "Your noble American has returned my Queen." "Nate has returned," she said. Her heart danced every time he returned to Sedonia. It's been a little over two years since Nate's been to Sedonia and she's curious to how long he's going to stay. The palace doors opened, and he entered. Sylvia stood up. He said, "Happy New Year's!" "Happy New Year's" she said, "and it's starting off in a great way." When they got close to one another, Sylvia fell into his arms. He kissed her like it's been a century since they've seen each other. When the kiss was over, she said, "Nate Patricks, you take my breath away." "Do I?" he asked. She nodded her head. "What I really want to do is take you away." "Take me away?" "Yes, to my world. That's why I'm here." Sylvia was taking a moment to answer. "I won't take no for an answer. We've planned this before remember?" "Okay, you talked me into it. When do we leave?" "Now. I know this is sudden, but I've been the one who's been patient." "Ready when you are," Sylvia said.

Sylvia had on an astronaut suit following behind Nate heading to the spacecraft. Before they got on the spacecraft, they waved to Mel, Harper, Wallace, and everyone else that was there. Sylvia and Nate got on and a few seconds later, the spacecraft took off. "I got to be stuck here with you," Wallace said. "Don't start," Mel said.

In space, Nate and Sylvia were floating around in the spacecraft. "This is amazing. I didn't know we could float in air," Sylvia said. "Only in space. There's no gravity or air in space. That's why we have to wear these space helmets so we can have oxygen and gravity is what keeps our feet planted on the ground in my world and yours." "Can you make love in space?" she asked. "I've never tried but I can blow you a kiss." He blew her a kiss and she blew the kiss back. "We should be near Earth now," Nate said. They got strapped down in their seats. "Is that Earth ahead of us?" "Yes." "I'm excited but nervous," Sylvia said. "You have nothing to worry about." "I know because I'll be with you." "Well, we're heading in," Nate said. They were greeted by fellow astronauts once they landed on base. "Nate, we didn't expect you back so soon," one named Cleotis, who was the captain. "I was in a hurry to get back so I could show you guys what I brought back." "Is there really life on another planet?" a female astronaut named Sammie asked. "I can show you better than I can tell you. Feast your eyes on this." Nate nodded for Sylvia to step out of the spacecraft. Once they've seen her, they were all wide-eyed. All the men definitely kept their eyes glued on her.

Sammie saw all the guys faces and made a comment, "What is it? You guys never seen a woman before?" "Where did she come from?" a man named Chad asked. "She's from the planet called Sedonia." "I don't believe she's from another planet. I think she's just some model. Something from another planet isn't going to look like that," Chad said. "Or she could be an alien disguised as a beauty Queen," Sammie said. "She is from another world. If anybody knows, I know. I've spent time in her world more than once." "How do you know you weren't brain washed or they erased your memory of what you really know?" Cleotis asked. "You can believe whatever you want. I know this woman is and she's here just to be with me." Nate drove Sylvia to his house in his Land Rover. "They don't like me," she said. "No, it's me," Nate said, "they don't believe me." They pulled in the driveway of a simple little house. "We're home," he said. "Wow this is certainly different," Sylvia said, when she stepped out of the Land Rover. As they were walking towards the house, Sylvia looked up at the sky. She was captivated by how high the palm trees reached the sky. She almost hurt her neck. Sylvia spun around in a circle looking at the surroundings. "Welcome to Los Angeles." Nate shows her around his house. "It may not be what you're used to, but it's cozy." "Your place is very nice, Nate." "I'm going to take you around town." "Maybe I should change," Sylvia said. "Right, you do want to fit in. That's why I bought some clothes so whenever I persuaded you to come here, you'll have something to wear." "I never had someone look out for me… I love you Nate." "I love you," he said. "I have to ask Nate, why do you come back to my world? There's lots of girls here." "Yeah, there's lots of girls and I've dated a few. When I first came to your world, I was a lost astronaut trying to get back home. I didn't know what to expect. I didn't expect to be shown so much love, so much honor, so much warmth. When I first met you and got know you, I didn't expect a great leader to be so vulnerable. You don't let being a leader go to your head. That's rare in this world. Finding real in the 21st Century is very rare also. So, if I have to go the distance to be with this love, I'll do that." Sylvia went to the bathroom to change into a simple gray, T-shirt and some dark blue jeans. Nate changed into a sweat suit. He took her nearby to some shops where clothing was sold. She enjoyed browsing at everything. Though she thought Earth people's clothes were unusual and different, she saw a dress that caught her eye. "I want to buy this," Sylvia said. "I'll buy it for you. They won't except your money." He bought the floral pink summer dress for her. "Something to show to the girls back home," Sylvia said. Then they went to a burger place where they could sit outside and eat. "You enjoying your burger and fries?" Nate asked. "Yes, it's delicious." "Tomorrow, I'll take you to some malls." "What's a mall?" "It's a place where there's different stores—like you can buy clothes, food, or go to the movies. We don't have to buy anything. We're just browsing." "I think

I like this world." There were two women that came to the counter of the burger joint. One of the women leaned over on the counter. She showed lots of cleavage and her breasts were pressing down on the counter. "Will you please get your tits off this counter," the cashier said. She stood up. Then he got a wet towel and wiped the counter off. "I'm sick of you damn hookers showing off your nastiness, spoiling everyone's appetite. People want to eat, not see all that." The hooker flipped the man off and the two women left. Sylvia witness what was going on and asked Nate, "What's a hooker?" "A woman who sells her body for money," he answered. "Why would a woman want to do that?" "Oh, everyone has their reasons." "Do all hookers dress the way those hookers do?" "Most of them," he said. "This world has all kinds of people." "Where are we going next?" "We're going to heard back home. It's getting late. We'll do more tomorrow."

Sylvia was just waking up in bed on a Saturday morning. Nate just came from the bathroom when he finished shaving. She was sitting up in bed when he stood by her bedside. He was shirtless, showing off that small bed of hair on his chest. He had his hands in his pockets of his pajama's bottoms. Nate bend down to kiss her. "Good morning," he said. "Good morning. It's so great to be kissed in the morning," she said. "I'm so glad you're here, Sylvia." He sat next to her on the bed.

"I can't believe we're from two different worlds, but we're so connected. I never felt this way before." Sylvia could see tears coming into his eyes. She placed both her hands on his face and kissed him. "I don't want you to leave," Nate said. "We'll see," Sylvia said. "How about some breakfast?" he asked. "Yes, I am hungry." "I bet you are. We're going to need something to restore our energy from all that love making last night." "Let's cook up something," she said. "I'll do the cooking. You just lay back and relax," he said. "Nate, you don't have to treat me like a Queen. Right now, I want to be ordinary." "Just relax. I got it." Sylvia lies back in bed while Nate cooks breakfast. While she was resting, the 32" flat screen Tv that was in the room, automatically came on. Nothing but static at first. Then Sylvia heard someone calling her name. It was a woman's voice. She rose up in bed. Even though the voice wasn't that clear, but it was vaguely familiar. After the voice said her name a couple more times, the picture came clear. "You didn't forget about me did you Sylvia?" "Leave me!" Sylvia screamed. Nate rushed to the bedroom. "You okay baby?" He sat on the bed. She had a horrified look on her face. "Veel… Veel is after me." "Veel," he said, not understanding. Sylvia pointed at the TV. The TV was off. "I don't understand what you're telling me. "Veel was on TV and was talking to me." "You sure you weren't having a nightmare?" "I did dose off for a moment." "That's all it probably was just a nightmare," he said, "oh, let me get back to the kitchen… the eggs might burn."

Nate and Sylvia went to mall Saturday afternoon. They talked and looked in different stores. After forty minutes of browsing, they got some Orange Julius pina coladas from the food court. They sat down for a moment. Sylvia was enjoying her pina colada, Nate was too busy looking around to enjoy his. "Is something wrong? You've been looking around ever since we've been here." "I have a feeling we're being watched," he said. "Who could be watching us?" "I don't know." "It's got to be Veel! I knew it wasn't a nightmare," Sylvia said. "Veel is dead. You defeated her." "Well, she's haunting me in the afterlife," she said. "I know we'll find out, even if we don't find out today," he said. "Nate, take me dancing." "Like to a club?" he asked. "Yes." "I stopped going to clubs a long time ago and I certainly don't want men looking at you. We can dance the night away at home." They ordered pizza from Pizza Hut and bought some cheap cherry wine from the liquor store. Then they got comfee on the couch to watch the movie, "The Hobbit." They ate half the pizza by the time the movie was over. Then they went to the bedroom to strip down out of their clothes. He picked her up, kissed her and she wrapped her legs around him. They fell back into the bed. Just when they were about to get into making love, Nate realized he left the shades up. He quickly pulled them down. An hour later, they both took a shower. Nate wrapped a towel around his waist and Sylvia had a towel around herself. She began rubbing coca butter lotion on when Nate said, "I think we're being watched here too, and I think someone's been in this house. I've never left my shades up." "Are you sure?" Sylvia asked. "I just have this feeling. I've been having this feeling ever since I brought you here." "Maybe I should go back to my world." "No, not yet. There's so much more I want to show you." "What are we doing now?" she asked. "Get a good night's sleep." "I don't want to go to sleep now… I want to go for a ride." "It's getting late Sylvia. Besides I want to take you to church in the morning and so I can see you in that pretty dress."

They went to a Baptist church that was a fifteen- minute drive. The place was already crowded even though they arrived ten minutes early. Nate and Sylvia sat in one of the middle pews. Nate took an envelope from where the envelopes were kept in the back of each pew. He started filling the envelope out. "What's that?" Sylvia asked. "A tithing envelope. This is people who pay a certain percentage of their income. It's like giving back to God what he's given to you." Nate takes his wallet out and puts a twenty-dollar bill in the envelope. "Too bad my money is no good," Sylvia said. "This is our money. When it's offering time, I'll let you put the money in the basket, but we'll walk up together. Your people don't do these kinds of things?" "No, we just pray and worship." "Do you pray to a certain kind of God?" he asked. "No, I pray to my ancestors and I look to the Kings and Queens who reigned before me. The one thing I've learned about the people here on Earth that I don't understand, since there's supposed to be only one God, why do people here have different beliefs?" "I would say some people were brought up on different beliefs. Like I was brought up Baptist. But the way to get in heaven is by reading the bible every day and living by those words." The service began exactly at eleven o' clock. Everybody got up and sang along with the choir. The choir sang a few more songs, then the announcements. When it was offering time, Nate gave Sylvia the tithing envelope and when it was their turn to go up, she dropped the money in the offering basket. Giving was always something she loved doing but giving money to someone you've never seen? The service lasted only an hour and a half. They headed back home when church service was over. "I made plans for us to go to eat," Nate said. "That sounds great," Sylvia said, not sounding too happy. "But first I have to make a run right quick." He leaves out in a hurry. She didn't want to go out to eat even though she was kind of hungry. Sylvia wanted to grab something to eat and go out for a joy ride in LA. She wasn't seeing all what she wanted to see. She wasn't looking to go to some fancy restaurant or any restaurant. She feasted all the time in her home. She was adventurous person. She always wanted to see something new. Sylvia hated to think the man she's in love with wasn't an exciting person. She was at the point that she was going to do what she wanted to do. Sylvia changed into some jeans and a T- shirt. She left a note she had written for Nate. She had to leave before he got back because Nate wouldn't let her out of his sight if she stayed. Sylvia left the house and hurried down the street. There were two people on the bus stop, and they were about to get on the city bus that was coming. She got on the bus behind the two people. "Where does this bus go?" Sylvia asked the bus driver. "Where are you trying to go?" the bus driver asked. "In the city." "You mean like Inglewood, Compton…" "Yeah, either one," she said. Sylvia was about to sit down. "Wait a minute," the bus driver said, "that will be a dollar fifty. She knew she couldn't use her money, so she used the extra money Nate gave her. Sylvia rode the bus for twenty minutes. She saw an area she wanted to check out. Sylvia ended up in a rough looking neighborhood. It was Mexicans and so-called blacks hanging out in front of some run-down apartments. She was interested in how people lived. Sylvia was walking through, some of the Mexicans guys were eyeballing her. She thought they were interested in talking to her, so she walked up to them to say hello. "What's a hot thing like you doing over here?" one of them asked. "I'm Sylvia, I'm from the planet Sedonia… I'm just visiting. The Mexican guys looked at each other. "Did she just say she was from another planet?" one of them asked the other. "It sounded like it to me," the other answered. They walked away from her and one said, "yep she's a weirdo alright or either on something." Sylvia walked on. A young black woman was pushing a baby stroller with a one-year-old girl in it and another little girl walking beside her. They were coming toward her. She stopped the woman.

"Hello, I'm Sylvia." Sylvia held her hand out. The woman looked at her hand, then looked at her.

"Are you one of those Jehovah Witnesses?" the woman asked.

"What?"

"It's always Jehovah Witnesses coming around here."

"No ma'am, I'm not."

"It's not good to be so quick to shake hands with people around here."

The woman walked away. Since Sylvia could see she wasn't welcome around here, she caught another bus.

Nate came out of the floral shop with a bouquet of pink roses. He passed by a newspaper stand before he was about to get in his Range Rover. Nate caught what the front page of the Los Angeles Times read… "Astronaut Nate Patricks is having a romantic affair with an alien from another planet that's in human form." Underneath that statement was a picture of him and Sylvia nude, kissing and touching. Certain parts of their body were blocked out for young viewers. Nate put money in the newspaper stand and took a newspaper out. He took a closer look at the picture. That picture was shot through his bedroom window. He knew all along they were being watched. Nate was mad and embarrassed. That picture was probably all over the internet. He got in his ride to head back home.

Sylvia was in Hollywood walking down the Hollywood Walk of Fame. She was admiring all the famous names she walked upon. Sylvia kept smiling at the fact she was enjoying herself. People were looking at her, but she would keep smiling at everyone that walked past her.

When Nate got home, he caught some people hiding out behind bushes across the street. He seen they had cameras. Nate came towards them. One of them said, "Oh wait, the alien is not with him."

"So, you want to spy on me again." He came even closer.

"Let's get out of here! He's probably contaminated!" They ran off.

"Go take pictures of some well- known celebrities and leave me alone!" he yelled out.

Nate went inside his home with the bouquet of roses. He looked around for Sylvia. When he couldn't find her, he called her name. The house remained quiet.

Sylvia ended up finding her way to Venice beach. She stood and watched people hustle, skateboarding, roller skating, showing off their bodies and doing many other exciting activities. All she could think about was how hungry she was. Sylvia saw some food stands where she could get something to eat. She got a cheeseburger; mozzarella sticks and a diet coke.

Sylvia sat at a picnic table and ate her food. Then she sat down in the sand by the shore, when she was done eating. It was so many people on the beach but the one thing that captivated her was looking out into that big blue ocean. Remembering in her world the ocean was pink. Her mind drifted off into thinking how different this world was from her world. It was so many different sorts of people… and their personalities were different. In Sedonia, the people weren't that much different from one another.

"Excuse me," a woman came up to her and asked, "aren't you that alien that Nate Patricks brought from another planet?"

It was that female astronaut Sammie from the other day.

"I've seen you guys' picture all over the internet."

She showed Sylvia the nude picture of them two on her cell phone on you tube. Sylvia got up and said," I got to go."

"There she goes," Sammie pointed her out.

It was news reporters and camera people following her. A lady news reporter tried to get Sylvia to talk to her.

"Is it true that you're really from another world?"

She held the microphone up to Sylvia. Sylvia just ran. She kept running and didn't look back.

It took two hours for her to get back to Nate's house. It was almost night- time and she almost forgot how to get back.

"Thank God," Nate said, "I've been searching the area for hours… where have you been?"

"I've been all over LA… glancing at different things. I hung out at the beach and I got ran off the beach by news people and paparazzi."

"You shouldn't have gone anywhere without me."

"I know I was anxious to see more."

"So, paparazzi harassed you at the beach?"

"Yes," Sylvia answered.

"They've also been the ones watching us throughout the time we've been seen together."

"I think of few of your astronaut friends have been telling those people that I'm an alien."

"They're no friends of mine if they're going to insult someone I care about." She hugged him.

"Maybe it was a mistake to bring you here."

"No, it wasn't. You didn't know it was going to turn out this way. I enjoyed my time here."

"I think it's time to take you back home… if you're ready to go back?"

"Yes, I'm ready to go back."

They headed to the base to board the spacecraft. They took off within minutes. They whipped through space like a shooting star and made it back to Sedonia in no time and they landed on the beach.

"It's so quiet here and the sun is still setting," Sylvia said, after they got off the spacecraft.

"No one knows we're here," Nate said.

"They weren't expecting me until tomorrow," she said.

"You know this scenery brings back memories when I first crash landed on this world. I hate to say good-bye again, but I will be back, my Queen."

"My King," she said.

They kissed and held each other for a long time. So long, they wanted to do it right there on the sand. Nate had to leave so he let go and got on the spacecraft and didn't look back. He hated seeing the tears in her eyes. Sylvia watched the spacecraft take off and disappear in the sky. She kept staring at the sky even when the stars appeared. She didn't want to go to her home right now or anyone knowing she was here. She wanted to stay right where she was and remember this night.

STILL ON THE THRONE

The Queen, Sylvia, was standing on the rooftop of her home, in pouring rain, dressed like she was ready for a war with her sword at her side. She had a grip on the sword, waiting. It was hard to see through the blinding rain, but soon enough, here comes the enemy, towards her. The enemy stops and stares at her with evil in their eyes. Veel pulls out two knives from under her black cloak.

"I'm going to slice you and dice you into the littles pieces," Veel said.

"That's not going to happen," Sylvia said, then she pulls out her sword.

With no hesitation, Veel came at Sylvia with the knives. Sylvia knocked one of the knives out of her hand with the quickness of her sword. Veel came of her again with the one knife. She missed because Sylvia jumped back. Veel kept swinging the knife at her but kept missing. The many times she swung the knife at Sylvia and missed, Veel did end up slicing her in the side. That wasn't going to stop Sylvia. She raised her sword at Veel. She knocked the sword out of her hand. Sylvia was pressing down on her wound with her hand. The rain was coming down even harder and everything was getting even darker for Sylvia. She fell down and was about to pass out from losing blood. Veel kneeled down beside her.

"Don't lose your head over this," Veel said and came at her with the knife.

Sylvia woke up and she was in her bedroom. Not out in the rain in some battle. She was attacked with another bad dream. A beautiful sunshine was coming in her window. As tired as she was, Sylvia started her day. She didn't realize how late in the day it was until she sat down at the dining room table and her housekeeper, Sonie said, "Hello my Queen… late start?"

"No, I just wanted to lie in bed a little longer today," Sylvia answered.

Sonie helped Amu the chef cleans up after breakfast, but made sure Sylvia got her breakfast which was cinnamon oatmeal, three strips of well-done bacon and a buttered biscuit, with apple juice. This was her breakfast every morning. She picked up her spoon to eat her oatmeal. Then she felt herself dosing off. She tried to fight off the sleeping spell by eating and not have her face end up in the oatmeal. Sylvia snapped out of the spell when someone screamed her name.

"I was wondering when you were coming to eat your breakfast, because I've been waiting for you," Mel said.

"Yeah, I was really tired."

"You haven't been energetic or yourself lately."

Mel sat across from her.

"Sylvia you're more than just a Queen to me, you're also my friend. You can talk to me."

"I'm alright, I just need more sleep."

"Then get back into bed."

"I can't right now…"

"Go back to bed," he told her. "You have nothing to worry about. Even the Queen needs a break and you need your beauty sleep." "Ok I'll finish my breakfast and I'll go back to bed." Mel gets up I'll go back to bed." Mel gets up and touches her on the shoulder and smiles at her before he walks away.

Sylvia went back to her bedroom but refused to sleep. For several months she's been having horrifying nightmares. In those several months she's hasn't really slept. Her people have noticed the changes in her moods and appearance. It started right after the last time she seen Nate. Every time she'd shut her eyes at night, Veel appeared. It was like a horror movie. Once the lights went out, Veel was trying to find a different way to destroy her. But she did remember Veel appearing the first in her dream when she was with Nate back in California. That must have been a sign that she was coming back for her. Veel was dead. She put an end to her, or did she?

She summoned Mel and a couple of guards to take her to Veel's grave. "What for?" Mel asked. "I want to make sure that witch is dead," she answered. "We all saw her die," Mel said. "I'm not so sure," Sylvia said. Mel thinks she's losing it. The graveyard was a long way from the palace. Nobody thought Veel deserved a descent burial. Sylvia first thought was to throw her body in the ocean but she's not a cold-hearted person. Besides the ocean was too clean of a place to dispose a corpse and let it deteriorate there. When they reached the gravesite, the workers there, dug up her casket. Then they opened the casket. There she was, her remains, bones, and in her clothing. "I hope this all you wanted to see. Now can we get the heck out of here?" Mel said. They put her back where she belonged and went home. Sylvia changed into one of her fabulous attires to sit on the throne. She still was extremely tired but wouldn't get any sleep. She sat there with her head down and one hand covering her face. "Sylvia, I thought you said you were going to get some sleep?" Mel asked when he entered the throne room. "I don't want to go to sleep." "Will you please get yourself some sleep! You look like you haven't slept in a year!" Fine," she said. Sylvia got up. Mel left the room. Sylvia began walking down the steps in front of her chair then she felt herself getting light-headed and dizzy. On the last step she fell forward on the floor and her crown rolled across the floor. It kept rolling until it hit the wall and landed flat like a coin. No one was in the throne room when this happened. A minute later, one of the spa room girls came in and saw the Queen lying very still on the floor. She screamed loud. Mel, Harper, Wallace and some others came running.

Everyone stood around Sylvia's bed in her bedroom while she was in a deep sleep, waiting to hear the reason why she collapsed, from the doctor. "She's extremely exhausted," the doctor said, "her body's finally getting the rest she needs." "She told me she's been having trouble sleeping…. do you know what could have been keeping her from her rest?" Mel asked the doctor. "I can't say. Maybe we'll find out when she wakes up," the doctor said. "How long she's gonna be asleep?" Harper asked. "For a long time, hours but she should be alright once she wakes up but if something changes, I'll be back." After the doctor left everyone stood there not knowing what to think. "Let's let the Queen sleep in peace," Mel said. Sylvia was left alone in her room with the lights turned out, sleeping away. A few moments ticked by and Sylvia gradually opened her eyes. She looked around the room. Since she realized she was in her bed. It was dark in her room, but Sylvia could tell someone, or something was lying in bed next to her. She reached over to the lamp that was next to her bed on a night- stand. It looked like a woman fully clothed in black and she was faced away from Sylvia. Then Veel looked over her shoulder at Sylvia. "No, not you again!" Sylvia said. Veel disappeared but reappeared, sitting at the foot of her bed. She had her back to Sylvia then looked over her shoulder at her. "Hope you've gotten enough sleep because your nap time is over. Veel stood up and faced her then Veel began floating in the air. Sylvia was freaking out as the evil spirit floated above her, staring her dead in the face, with black marbled eyes. "You stay away from me you witch! Stay away!" Mel was not far from Sylvia's room when he heard her screams. He rushed into the room. Sylvia was staring up at the ceiling. "Sylvia," he said as he grabbed hold of her. Veel was still in a horizontal position, staring down at her from the ceiling but then she disappeared. "Mel," Sylvia cried then she buried her face in his chest. "What happened?" he asked. She lifted her head and looked passed him. "She's behind you!" she said in a nervous tone. Mel turned around. "I don't see anything." "She's there, she's there," Sylvia replies. "I tell you I don't see anything," he said. "She's the reason why I can't sleep. I'm the only one that can see her. She's staring at me with a wicked smile on her face right now. She's trying to drive me into insanity." "Is there something I can do, or anyone can do?" "I wish I could pray this witch away… that's it… the power of prayer," she said. "Prayer always changes things. Will you pray with me?" "How could I say no," Mel answered. The lamp on the night-stand fell on the floor. Mel jumped up. "I felt something move passed me real fast," he said. "It was her. I can't see her now, but I know she's still here.

That's right witch, with the power of prayer you will no longer interfere with my rest." They both kneeled at her bedside and prayed.

Mel explained Sylvia's situation to the people after they prayed. Mel thought it be a good idea if everyone prayed with her at her bedside. So, everyone did. With the prayers and love filling the room, it put Sylvia's mind at ease. She was able to roll over and fall asleep. Everyone left the room feeling at ease themselves knowing their Queen will get the proper rest she needs. Mel was the last to leave the room and he said, "Sleep well my Queen."

Sylvia was able to sleep for six hours straight. When Veel showed up during her nap time, Veel would have no expression on her face. Sylvia would peacefully be still asleep, then Veel vanished. She promised herself to pray always to keep the witch out of her life forever. Now Sylvia was ready to get out of bed. Once her feet touched the floor, Sonie came in. "No, no, no, my Queen… where are you going?" "Just to the bathroom, then down to the kitchen." "You must not leave this room. Take care of your business in the bathroom but get back into bed." Sonie started fluffing her pillows. "I haven't eaten since breakfast. We're got you covered," Sonie said and she went out in the hallway. She and the chef rolled in a silver cart. He lifted the lid off what was on the silver cart. Well done steak and mashed potatoes with brown gravy on a silver platter. The look and the smell made Sylvia's stomach growl even more. On a second cart was a bottle of cherry wine chilled in a bucket of ice. "Last but not least, a big slice of your favorite dessert, coconut cake." The piece of cake was on a plate next to the wine. "You guys are too much," Sylvia said. "Nothing's too much for our Queen," Sonie said. "Enjoy your meal and we'll be back for the dishes." "Thank you," Sylvia said.

Sylvia got nothing but rest for a whole week. She got served breakfast, lunch and dinner every day by her bedside. She prayed every night and every morning, thanking the God of the universe for the love that surrounds her and keeping the demons away so she can sleep. Sylvia knew she could count on her people to take care of things while she remained in her room. Some nights before she went to bed, she would gaze out her window at that beautiful ocean afar and allow that breeze to blow in her face. What a peaceful world I live in she would say to herself. Unlike the planet Earth that her Nate was from. On her big screen TV in her room and she's only been watching in the past week, CNN and world news. All the violence, murders, racism, rapes, child molestation, and bullying in schools going on Earth. She's only had to deal with evil leaders in her world. In this world there was never bad news. Every day was a great day on planet Sedonia. People disagreed or had an argument, but no one died or got hurt over something petty. A new week has come around and Sylvia woke up bright and early on a Sunday morning. She was very well rested and ready to be back on the throne. She washed her face, brushed her teeth with her electric toothbrush then she put on a simple outfit. After that, the Queen hurried down to the kitchen for her breakfast. Sonie and the chefs, Amu and Lunia, had just begun cooking breakfast. They were so busy they didn't know Sylvia was there in the kitchen. "Good morning," the Queen said. "Oh, hello my Queen, breakfast will be ready in a little while," Sonie said, but didn't say anymore to her. Her chef stayed quiet like always, stirring the pancake batter. Sylvia went to the dining room to have a seat. Harper was there placing dishes and silverware on the table. "Oh, Sylvia nice to see you but I got to go help in the kitchen." He hurried off. That was odd to her. She and Harper always had something to talk about. She just sat there quietly. Here came Mel and Wallace. "Sylvia whatcha doing up so early?" Wallace asked. "What are you two doing here so early? I never see either one of you until after nine o' clock," Sylvia said. Mel and Wallace looked at each other. "Sylvia I'd like to talk to you out in the hallway," Mel said. She and Mel step out in the hallway. "Are you going to tell me why everyone's acting so strange?" she asked. "Yes, it's just that while you've been resting, we all recently found out some tragic news." "What tragic news?" "We found out Nate died." "What!" Sylvia yelled. "He was in space in his spacecraft and it ended up hitting a meteor--- his spacecraft blew up." "How did you find out about this?" she asked. "It came on the news late in the evening." She was in shock and didn't know what to do." "I'm so sorry my Queen. Nobody didn't know how to face you and tell you. I knew I had to be the one." Her heart started to pound very hard, her chest was hurting. She turned away from Mel to walk away. Then she ran to her room and fell into her bed and soaked her face in her pillow. Wallace came in the hallway and said, "Maybe we should see about her." "Let her be alone," Mel said. Sylvia cried off and on for hours. She didn't leave her room. At one point, she turned on her TV. The same disturbing news on all the news channels. The news she still hoped wasn't true about Nate popped up. There was a candlelight vigil in his hometown Long Beach, California, in his memory. Sylvia turned her TV off and she stayed in bed. Then evening came and Sonie came in her room. Sylvia was lying in bed, staring up at the ceiling. "My Queen, would you like something to eat? I've noticed you haven't eaten all day. I don't want nothing to eat." Sonie left. She was too heart- broken to anything else. A couple hours passed by and Sylvia was able to drift off to sleep. A gentle hand touched her face. She opened her eyes. It was kind of dark in her room but when the person spoke her name, she knew automatically. Sylvia turned on her light. She knew she had to be dreaming. At least it wasn't a nightmare. "This can't be real," she said. "Yes, it's really me," Nate said. "How could it be? I was told you were dead. I saw the candlelight vigil on TV." "Everyone thought I was dead. My spacecraft did blow up in space on my way here. I ended up hitting a meteor head on, but I was able to escape before my spacecraft went to pieces. I strapped on my rocket and parachute so I could get to your world quick and land safely. "How long have you been here?" she asked. "Since this morning. That ride was long, and it wore me out. I've been passed out on the beach for a while." Sylvia just stared at him like he was a ghost. "I know this seems like a shocker but it's really me." "I know but I'm glad you're here. But when you're ready to leave, how are you going to get back home?" "I wasn't planning on going back home." "You're going to stay here permanently?" "Yes, if you'll let me." "You know I want you here more than anything but what about your family, your friends?" "They know I'm in a better place." "Yes, you're in a much better place," Sylvia said. "Since I'm going to be sticking around, I think it's time you have a King by your side." He showed her a little box with a ring in it. "So, are you asking me?" He got down on one knee. "Will you?" he asked. "Yes, definitely. I've also been doing some thinking." Nate stood up. "What have you been thinking about? I was thinking about making some changes in my kingdom, in this world." "Why? This a perfect world." "There's no such thing. This world has many flaws." "What kind of changes?" "Like the night spots for instance. The women are no longer going to work nude. They're going to be fully clothed. No more exotic dancers. The menu is going to change too. The names of the food items and drinks are going to change also. Only non-alcohol beverages are going to be served all restaurants." "What made you want to make these changes?" "These erotic places should have never existed. My enemies have opened these businesses. When Alijal was here, and when the Kings and Queens before him reigned, there was no kind of fornication or provocative public places. It was the law and it's going to be a new law here in my home." "I can't wait to hear this one," Nate said. "No more body massages. I the men like to make out with the masseuses." "What will happen if anyone breaks these rules?" "They will be exiled, forced to leave this planet." "I see you've finally started thinking like a leader," Nate said. "Yes, this my world and it was time to set the laws." "It's time you became my wife." "What are we waiting for?" Sylvia asked.

The wedding was prepared in three days. The colors were white and silver. Sylvia's best friend Magalina, who got married three years ago, was going to be Sylvia's maid of honor and Mel was going to be the best man. The wedding scene was so beautiful that day, not because of the colors but because of the many tears of joy that was shed. Sylvia was a Queen that was so loved, and everyone loved their new King. It was time for a King to take that seat on that throne. After the wedding was a great wedding feast. This was a day of happiness and fulfillment for her as everyone held up their glasses for a toast of their new King. This moment made Sylvia think back to when she began her reign as the modern Queen.

ALL THE QUEEN'S MEN

She looked into his eyes and he looked into her eyes before they shared a loving kiss. This was their first night as husband and wife in their glamourous suite they got for they're honeymoon. Nate picked her up and carried her to the bed. As Sylvia was lying on the bed, he was admiring the white lingerie she had on but was going to be coming out of it in a moment. Sylvia was admiring her husband's flawless body also. He wore nothing but some silk white pajamas pants. Then they made love until they were too tired. They both laid on their stomachs after they made love. Nate was facing her, but Sylvia was faced away from him. "That was great. So much passion," Nate said as he rubbed her back. "I can't believe we actually belong to each other now." Sylvia wasn't saying anything. "Is something wrong?" he asked. "I was just thinking about how it was with my first husband." "Why are you thinking about him?" "How he left me to rule over this great world but, he treated me as second." "That's the past and to me you've always been number one," Nate said. "Same here," Sylvia said. Sylvia and Nate returned to the palace four days later. They came in from the back entrance because they didn't want anyone to know they have returned yet. They crept through the hallway where the bedrooms were. "You can put the suitcases in my room," she said. "It's our room now," Nate said. "Yes, I'm going to head to the throne room." "And I'll unpack our things," he said. She gave him her loving smile and he smiled back. As she was heading to the throne room, Sylvia could tell her people were there waiting on her. Once she stepped into the throne room, her people were standing around some individuals that weren't from this world. She recognized them immediately from the trip she made to Earth. They all had Nasa uniforms on and seeing them put Sylvia in an unpleasant mood. They didn't make her feel welcome on their planet and something told her they're here to start something. "My Queen, you're here," Mel said. All her people turned around and looked when he said that. "What's going on here?" Sylvia asked. "Pardon me your majesty," one of the male astronauts named Cleotis began, "We're not here to intrude. We're on a mission to find an astronaut named Nate Patricks." The astronauts then recognized her. "Haven't we met before?" Cleotis asked. "You thought I was an alien," Sylvia said. "Nate has always claimed he travels to a planet that none of us has ever heard of. On Earth, family members and friends, believes he's dead. We wanted to make sure his death was true by finding this planet and making sure this planet exists and he's not hiding out here." "He's not hiding out here," Sylvia said. "That's right this is my home now," Nate said when he came in the throne room. All the astronauts were shocked. Nate you're alive!" Sammie said.

"And you said he wasn't hiding out here," Chad, the other astronaut said. "I know what I said, and didn't you hear him say this is his home now?" "How could you abandon your home on Earth and have everyone think you're dead and live on another planet?" Cleotis asked. "Because I'm happier here." "Your family is going to be disappointed when they find out you're still alive." "You don't worry about my family." "We're going to tell them you're alive and we spoke to you. They have a right to know." "Listen here," Sylvia said, cutting in, "I didn't cause any problems when I came to your world, don't cause problems on mine." "We're not here to cause problems," Cleotis said. "You don't have to tell them, I'll just go back to Earth, Nate said. "We can head out now if you're ready," Cleotis said. Nate went back to the bedroom to pull out his Nasa uniform that he thought he'd never had to wear again. "Are you sure about going back to Earth with them?" Sylvia asked. "No, I'm not sure, but I do think I should see my family, but I'll be back." "How do you know they'll bring you back?" "I don't know," he said. "This doesn't sound right. I'm coming with you." "No Sylvia." "I should meet your family. I didn't get to the last time I went to California with you." "You shouldn't come." "I'm going no matter what you say. I don't want to lose you." He holds her tight. "You're not going to lose me. We're always going to be together… I promise." They all boarded the spacecraft immediately that was only a few minutes from the palace. Mel, Magalina, and Strew accompanied Sylvia and Nate to the spacecraft. "Hurry back," Magalina said. "I will," Sylvia said, and she blew them all a kiss good-bye before they sealed the spacecraft door. They got ready for take- off. Once they took off, they ended up in space in no time. Cleotis stopped the spacecraft in the middle of space. ''Why have we stopped?" Nate asked. All of them pulled out guns on Nate and Sylvia. "What is this?" Nate asked. "Change of plans… well it was never our intention to seeing you back to Earth," Cleotis said. "I knew one day you were going to leave Earth for good and pull a stunt like you did to do it. You've shown many hints that you were. Ever since you made that trip out here in space and got lost, it's made me curious what you kept coming back here for." Cleotis looked at Sylvia. "What this alien have must be good for you to keep passing up all the millions and billions of women on Earth." "You know I am not an alien, and neither are my people. We're ordinary people that live differently," Sylvia said. "And you don't have a clue about the relationship I have with this woman and her people," Nate said. "Well, I would like a place in this world of yours--- on the throne." "The throne is no place for you," Sylvia said. "I'm going to make a place for myself, so you're no longer the ruler." "I will not allow you to corrupt my world or my people." "You won't be able to stop me because I have the gun and you're both are going to be dead in a moment." Cleotis opens the door then comes behind Nate with the gun towards his back. "Move!" he said to

Nate. He and Nate move to the door. "What do you expect me to do?" Nate asked. "Jump," Cleotis said. "Why don't you just kill me now?" Nate turned slowly but then quickly pushed him and Cleotis fell back on the other two men. He started picking up all their guns before they got back up on their feet. "Not so fast," Sammie said. She had her gun pointed towards Sylvia's head. Nate pulled Cleotis up by the arm and pointed his gun at him. The other two men picked up their guns and they aimed at Nate. "Shoot me and it will be the end of Captain Cleotis." Sylvia elbowed Sammie in one of her breasts as hard as she could. "Ouch!" she screeched. "Do you know how much these implants costs me?" "I'm not trying to guess." Sylvia took her gun from her and pointed it at her. "Now it's time for you to drop your weapons," Nate told the other two. "No release them or you're dead," Chad said. "Go ahead and shoot them!" Sammie screamed. "Shut your ass up," Cleotis said. The men fired at the same time. Nate and Sylvia shielded themselves with Cleotis in front of him and Sammie in front of Sylvia. A bullet hit Sammie in her other breast and a bullet hit Cleotis in the stomach. They felt guilty shooting the wrong people. "Drop your weapons or I'm going to shoot," Nate said. The men dropped their weapons. "What are you going to do now, throw us all out the door?" Cleotis asked, barely able to speak. "I'm not the person you are." Sylvia helped Cleotis and Sammie patch up their wounds from a first aid until they're able to get medical care. Nate tied up the two men so they couldn't try anything. Then he took spacecraft off auto pilot and took over. "We're on our way to Earth."

The two male astronauts were taken to jail soon as they arrived on Earth. Cleotis and Sammie were taken to the hospital but are going to end up in jail after they're released from the hospital. Nate made sure no news reporters knew about him being alive. He wanted his parents to be the first to know before the public. He and Sylvia disguised themselves by wearing sunglasses and wigs and cheap attire. They caught the city bus to Nate's house. His Land Rover was still there in the driveway. Everything in the house remained the same, the way he left it. Then he wanted to drive to his parents' house, but he didn't want to startle them. They got back on the city bus, even though they could have walked because his parents' home wasn't that far. They had a gray Cadillac that was in the driveway. Nate's heart was beating heavy as he and Sylvia stood at the doorstep of his parents' house. "Are you ready for this?" Sylvia asked. "Yes, I'm here and it's best that they know." He pushed the doorbell and his heartbeat even faster when he heard the footsteps coming to the door. "Who is it?" a woman's voice asked. Nate almost said, "Mama," but he was able to say, "Ma'am, I'm a close friend of Nate's. I'm here to give my condolences." His Mom opened the door, but only halfway. "I'm so sorry Mrs. Patricks." He was going to keep pretending to be this other person but seeing his mother's face he didn't want to keep beating around the bush. Nate removed his sunglasses, fake beard and baseball cap. Once she saw that it was her beloved son, she wasn't standing up no more. He came in the house and kneeled down by his mother who laid passed out on the floor. Sylvia came in too, but just stood there. "Karen… Nate!" his father, Andrew said, when he came from the kitchen. Nate's younger cousin, Jennie followed right behind him. "Is that really you Nate?" Jennie asked. "Is this some kind of a joke?" Andrew asked. "No, it's really me Dad." Jennie had tears in her eyes. "We'd really thought you were dead," she said. "People claimed me dead." Karen woke from her fainting spell. "Are you really here?" she asked. Nate helped her to her feet. "Yes, I'm here Mama." He hugged her. "Where have you been all this time then?" Andrew asked. "I got married and I just finished my honeymoon." He put his arm around Sylvia. "This is my wife." Sylvia took off her sunglasses. "How come you'd never brought her around?" Karen asked. "And what's up with the wigs, the disguises?" Andrew asked, "Are you guys wanted?" "People think I'm dead and I wanted my folks to be the first to know that I'm not before everybody else knows." "I'm Jennie, Nate's favorite cousin." Jennie had her hand out to shake Sylvia's hand. "Nice to meet you," Sylvia said. "Where did you two meets?" Karen asked. "It's a long story. You wouldn't believe it, but it's a great story." "Are you and your family from here?" Karen asked, Sylvia. "Mom, Dad, we have to go." "When will you be back?" his Mom asked. "You will hear from me. Just know that I'm okay." Nate and Sylvia left his parents and went straight to the KTLA Channel 5 News station. Breaking news at five o' clock this evening: Astronaut that was claimed dead is alive and well! Nate spoke publicly with millions of viewers all over the world, watching. "The people I worked with at Nasa, claimed me dead. I just was lost in space. They came and found me and brought me back home. I just thought everyone should know that I'm alive, but I want to move on with my life in peace." His speech was all over social media and various TV channels. He was still hounded by some news reporters when he and Sylvia was leaving the news station. "So, what's your next step in life?" a lady reporter asked. "Living peacefully and privately like I said before." Nate's parents and other family members had watched him on TV while he made his speech. His family was proud that he wanted to keep his life private. Nate and Sylvia went back to his house. They've haven't eaten all day, so he ordered a large supreme pizza from Pizza Hut and had it delivered. The little bit of food he had in his refrigerator he threw out because it had spoiled while he's been gone. While they ate the pizza and drank some Pepsi, Sylvia began asking, "Are we going back to Sedonia?" "Yes, tomorrow evening. I have to see my parents one more time and I have to sell this house. I'm sorry for what has happened to get me to come back home." "What do you mean? Sylvia asked. "I would have waited awhile to even come back here and tell everyone I'm alive. Well, I wouldn't have a way to get back here because my spacecraft was destroyed. Everything worked out even though it was an unpleasant ride to get here. I'm glad you came with me. I couldn't have done this alone." "We're in this together," Sylvia said. "We're sure are," Nate said. "I'm moving away," Nate says to his parents. He and Sylvia were sitting at his parents' kitchen table across from them. "Moving where?" Karen asked. "It's hard to explain. I'll be able to explain it to you soon. Just know that I'm alright. I'm saying good-bye for now. I'll call you when I get home… love you guys." Nate couldn't stick around in LA much longer. He wanted to avoid his parents' questions and other people's questions. He and Sylvia both stayed prisoners in his house until he was able to sell it. Three days on Earth was more than enough time to take care of what needed to be taken care of. They rode the bus to the Nasa base. They boarded the spacecraft and they put on the spacesuits. Before take-off, they held hands. "Let's go home," he said.

Sylvia and Nate put together a dinner for everyone in the palace once they returned to Sedonia. The King and Queen stood as everyone else stayed seated. Then Sylvia began her passionate speech. "I am so grateful to live in a world we live in. I'm having this dinner to show my gratitude to everyone here. Mel, you've been so good to me since the beginning. You've always showed me love and concern like a true friend should." Mel gave that proud smile of his. "Harper, you've always calmed me with your magnificent harp and you've always listened to me." Harper gave her a thumbs up. "Wallace… what can I say? You've always been Wallace but you're still a great guy." Wallace shows his charming smile. "Oh Magalina… I wouldn't be here if it wasn't for you. You and Strew I look up to both you guys." Magalina blew her a kiss, Strew, gave Sylvia a nod. "To my King, we were from two different worlds, but now we're one." "Nothing's gonna separate us," Nate said. Sylvia lifted her glass of wine in the air. "Here's to you my love and all you great men and to all the women here." Everyone now stood and lifted their glasses of wine. "To love," Sylvia said. "To love," everyone repeated and drank.

In the morning, Nate recorded himself, sending a message to his parents through face book. "Hello Mom and Dad! I know you're still wondering where I've gone… now I'm going to tell you. I'm living somewhere way different from California, well way different from Earth. I know you're asking what does he mean different from Earth? I found love and life on another planet. Yes, the people here are different from Earth. Sedonia is the name of this world and this world isn't run by presidents, mayors, or congressmen. This world is ruled by Kings and Queens. The woman that I told you that was my wife, is the Queen and I'm her King now. I'm a part of this world now but I'll never forget where I came from. I love you guys and the rest of the family. I'll always keep in touch and I'll always come back and visit." He posted pictures of some of the scenery in Sedonia and wrote, "another world, another place."

THE GIFT

It was that time of the year again when some people were out doing their early holiday shopping. Mel and Harper were the two out and about shopping but not for the Christmas season. The Queen's birthday was in a couple days and they were wanting to get the best gift for her possible. The birthday bash was going down this Saturday and everyone from all over was going to be attending. Mel was in the jewelry shop and a certain necklace caught his eye. Harper has been in different stores debating on what kind of gift to get. He wanted to get something that could be useful to her. He looked in an electronics store then he decided against electronics because that was something everyone had and used these days. Harper found an antique shop. It was so many interesting things in there to look at but something way back in the corner of the store really got his attention. When he got close up to what he was eyeing, he still didn't get what it was. "Excuse me sir," he asked the store clerk, "what is this?" The clerk came over to where he was. "It's a Lady-bot," the clerk answered. "A Lady-bot…you mean like a female robot?" "Yes." "What does she do? How does she work?" "She run on batteries and she has an on and off switch in her back. It's programmed to do whatever you like for her to do." "I've never seen nothing like this before. Are there many of these around?" "No, they're very rare. They were created nearly forty years ago, and they were made to be little helpers for especially for disabled people. Yes, this little lady has been here for a very long time. Nobody really needs them anymore," "Well I need it, how much for it?" "I'll give it to you for a good price." "Great!" Harper said. Mel met back up with Harper when he left out of the antique shop. "Wow, what you get?" Mel asked, when he seen the huge package that Harper had wrapped in pink silk. "Can't tell you. Wait until the party." "Well, I got the Queen this…" Mel opened a jewelry box with a white pearl necklace in it. "Very lovely," Harper said. "I guess we have what we came for," Mel said. "Yes sir," Harper answered. "Good, let's go home."

The birthday extravaganza was set to begin by seven, but people began showing up by two o' clock. The event was held in the ballroom of her castle and the place was decorated in perfection. Once seven o' clock struck, the ballroom was packed, and the event began with an orchestra playing a birthday tune. A few moments later, the Queen entered the room. A thunderous applause filled the room. The crowd was divided so she was able to walk upon the blue carpet laid out for her and to be seated in a fancy chair so she can kick back, relax, and enjoy her birthday. Mel stood on the right of her and Wallace stood on left of her once she was seated.

"Happy birthday to the Queen!" Harper said. "We all want you to kick your shoes off and get comfortable and get ready to be entertained." Sylvia just smiled. Up first were the spa room ladies. All four of them were in colorful outfits and began singing and dancing. After their fifteen- minute performance, the ladies handed Sylvia a beautifully wrapped present. She untied the present and pulled out a colorful cloth that was like a cape. "Happy birthday to our Queen," the ladies said. "This is lovely, very lovely," Sylvia said. She looked the beautiful cloth over and put it back in the box. Mel presented his gift. "Happy birthday my Queen," he said. Sylvia opened the gift. "Oh Mel, this is a beautiful necklace, thank you." "You're very welcome." He hugged her. "Happy birthday my Queen," Wallace said, and he handed her a bouquet of white roses. "Thank you," she said. He hugged her. There were many applauses for the ladies' performance and the gifts. "Now for my gift to the Queen," Magalina said. She handed Sylvia a box of perfume. "For my lovely friend." Magalina hugged her. "Anyone else have a present for the Queen?" Harper asked. No one came forward. "Everyone being here is the best gift of all," Sylvia said. "Oh yes, my Queen but this gift I have for you is also the best gift of all." One of the guards helped Harper bring forth the huge parcel wrapped in the pink silk wrap, tied up with pink ribbon. "I present to you… the gift," Harper said. Sylvia stood up. Her gift stood taller than she and she was anxious to know what was in this box and so was everyone else. Sylvia pulled off the ribbon and tore off the wrap. It revealed a brown paper box. She pulled off the lid. Sylvia was in aww and pulled her gift out of the box. "What is it? A robot or something?" Harper took away the box so everyone could see what it was. "Yes, it's a robot, a Lady-bot," Harper said. "I've never seen nothing like this. She has hair made of yarn," Sylvia said. "And she's made of aluminum. But what is she for, what does she do?" "Simple things, like make your bed for you, pick up your dishes. I thought it would be great for you because of your wrist injury." "That was very thoughtful, you're always thoughtful, Harper," she said. "She has a switch in her back to turn her off and on." Harper flicked her on and the robot began to light up. She lit up like a rainbow. Everyone was amazed. The Lady-bot came to life and asked, "Hello, what can I get for you?" Then everyone applauded. "This is amazing," Sylvia said. The birthday party continued with more music and everyone danced. Sylvia was also presented with an enormous birthday cake and she made a wish. "I hope I have many more great birthdays like this one." She blew out all forty-one candles.

Sylvia was lying in her bed, almost ready to turn in for the night. She wanted to stay up for the last thirty minutes of her birthday. She didn't want the day to end. She enjoyed it too much. All the love she got for her birthday, but it was one person she didn't get to see or hear from today. Just when she was thinking about that, a call was coming through on her telepad. Nate popped in video when she answered it. "How's my birthday girl doing?" he asked with a smile. "I'm excellent... too bad you're not here." "I tried to make it back there in time for your birthday, but it didn't happen, sorry sweetheart." "It's okay, all that matters you remembered--- when are you coming back?" "Tomorrow hopefully. How's your wrist?" he asked. "Still a little swollen but it's getting better. How come you're hardly ever here, Nate? I thought Sedonia was your home now?" "It is, I just have to keep checking up on my parents. Don't worry, I'll make it up to you for missing out on your birthday... take care," he said. "Take care," she said. Sylvia headed to the bathroom after talking to her husband. When she was on her way there, she glanced at the robot that stood by her balcony door. It was creepy looking, just standing there. It was going to be her little helper so Sylvia couldn't wait to see what the Lady-bot could really do.

Sylvia was riding along the beach on her white stallion. The day was very breezy but great for a day at the beach. The winds became stronger as she continued to ride. The winds really picked up and her stallion was startled, and she fell off. Sylvia sprained her wrist and was rolling in the sand, grasping on to her wrist, whining. She sat up quick, realizing she was in her bed. Sylvia looked at her bandaged wrist. The throbbing in her wrist is making her having nightmares of her accident on the beach days ago. It was almost daylight, but she was still going to get herself some good sleep. She rolled over in bed and opened her eyes and saw the Lady-bot standing over her. "Oh my," Sylvia said, sitting up. "Good morning your highness," Lady-bot said, "I have some water and some medicine to ease the pain in your arm." "Thank you," Sylvia said, taking the water and the two tablets from her. She drank her water and took her medicine. "I need to give you a name," Sylvia said, "You remind me of a raggedy Ann... not that you're raggedy. You have hair like yarn and you're unusual looking robot... so I'm going to call you Ann." "Thank you your highness," Lady-bot said. "Good afternoon your majesty," Sonie said, when she came in. "I hope you don't mind me borrowing your robot. I didn't want to disturb you while you were sleeping, and I needed the help in the kitchen." "It's perfectly okay," Sylvia said, "Her name is Ann now." "Well Ann, let's get all the dishes put away in the kitchen," Sonie said. "Would you still like some breakfast my Queen?" "I'll skip breakfast today, thank you." Sonie and Ann left her room."

Nate arrived in Sedonia a day later. He kisses his wife and gave her a rose. "I'm going to have to leave the day after tomorrow," he said. "Why, you just got here?" Sylvia said. "I know my parents insisted I come back for Thanksgiving." "I thought you said that Sedonia was your home now. It seems you're on Earth more than being here. Are you seeing somebody else and just using your parents as a reason to keep going back?" "No, why would

I have destroyed my spacecraft?" "But you have another spacecraft now." "Well, I want you to come back to Earth with me, so you spend Thanksgiving with my family." "I'm not doing that. We have huge feasts every year and it's the most important part of my life as the Queen." "Well, I have to go back home," he said. They didn't sleep together in the same room the two days he was there, and they didn't say much to each other either until he left again. She knew their marriage was in trouble.

That day, when Nate left, Sonie, Amu, Lunia, Ann and Sylvia began prepping for the feast. They had hundreds of people to feed so they always began cooking two days before the feast. Sylvia was pouring cake batter in the baking pan, but she almost dropped the bowl she was pouring the cake batter from. Sylvia put the bowl down on the counter. She began to cry and then ran out of the kitchen. Amu thought she was still having pain in her wrist; Sonie believes Sylvia is hurting behind her martial issues. Ann just continued cutting the jellied cranberry sauce. Sylvia ran to her room and laid down on her bed. She kept trying to wipe away her tears, but the tears kept flowing from the pain she was feeling in her heart. She couldn't bear to let anyone see her crying because of a man and she was the Queen. All her life, she's never been loved the way she wanted to be loved. Every guy that came in her life only wanted her by their side for their selfish reasons. It has gone on too long. It was time to be rid of him.

Sylvia returned to the kitchen and continued what she was doing. "Is everything alright your majesty?" Amu asked. "Couldn't be better," she said. Sonie was cutting bananas for the banana pudding; Amu was putting four pumpkin spice pies in the oven and Ann was still cutting the jellied cranberry sauce.

Ten hours in the kitchen, Sylvia was ready for a soak in the bathtub. While she was soaking, Ann fluffed her pillows for her that was on her bed. She relaxed in her bathtub not wanting to think about anything, especially not Nate.

After Sylvia finished her breakfast the next day, Nate called her, but she didn't answer. She had no time for him. Sylvia had more work to do on prepping up the remainder of the big feast. She and Ann went with Mel to the dining hall where the dinner was going to be held. The spa room ladies were setting the tables and decorating. "This always looks more and more beautiful each year," Sylvia said. "Very festive," Mel said. Mel, Harper, and Wallace helped out Sylvia and others in the kitchen that evening. With the extra help, they had the dinner done early. Everyone had some champagne after their hard work. Mel walked with Sylvia through the hall. She was ready to turn in for the night. "Be sure to get some good sleep tonight," Mel said. "All of us is going to need sleep," she said. "I know it's not my business, but I'm concerned about you," he said. "There's nothing to worry about. I'll be fine." "If you say so." He gives her a hug. "Goodnight," she said to him before he walked away. Ann was fluffing her pillows on her bed like every night when Sylvia came in the room. She checked her tele-pad and Nate has called a couple more times and left text messages. She erased it all. She was in a better mood and nothing was going to spoil it now. Sylvia took a quick shower and brushed her teeth. Then she got on her knees by her bed to say a prayer. "Ok Ann, it's time for all of us to get some sleep." "Yes, your majesty. It's been a pleasure to assist you, like always." "Night-night," Sylvia said. "Goodnight," Ann said. Sylvia switches her off then she sits her in a chair near her balcony door. Sylvia slides open the balcony door just a little for some of the cool night air to ease in. She felt the sleepiness come upon her. About thirty minutes after Sylvia went to sleep, Ann, who was still sitting in chair, in some way, rebooted herself and was switched on. She rose up out of the chair and walked straight over to Sylvia's bedside. Sylvia had her back to her but woke up from her sleep because she had a feeling someone was in her room. She sat up and looked around her bedroom. Nothing but quietness. She laid back down and went back to sleep. Ann was sitting in the chair like before Sylvia first went to bed.

The Queen awoke with happiness in her heart to another great day. She quickly got up to get dressed and beautify herself. Every year, it was her duty to look her best for hundreds of people who wanted to dine with the Queen. Once she got herself ready, Sylvia went to Ann to switch her on, but she noticed her robot was really warm. "Did I leave you on? I could have sworn I switched you off last night." Ann was turned off. She switched her on and the robot said, "Good morning your majesty… what can I do for you today?" "Let's hurry to kitchen then to the dining hall." In the kitchen was Sonie, quietly reading a book and keeping an eye on the little hens roasting in the oven. "Hi," Sylvia said, and she kept her voice at a low volume. "How much longer on the birds?" "Just an hour," Sonie answered, in a low volume also. "Well, I'm going to the dining hall to make sure everything's ready for the guest," Sylvia said. She heads to the dining hall and Ann follows her. Amu, Mel, Wallace, and Lunia brought in trays of food. There were three large tables and each table had to have more than enough amounts of food and beverage. Three hundred people were expected to arrive like every year and every year things had to be perfect. "Wow, everything looks wonderful," she said. Harper comes in. "The guests are starting to arrive." "Cool, let's start greeting the guests," Sylvia said. Sylvia, Ann, and Harper head to the throne room. The guard men opened the palace doors and the spa room ladies, began greeting the guests. Sylvia and Harper began greeting the guests too. Once all three hundred guests arrived, the feast began. All the guests took their seats in the dining hall but then the Queen had everyone stand and hold hands for grace. After the prayer, everyone was seated.

Everyone helped themselves to delicious dishes of food in front of them. Some had to pass the gravy or some rolls for someone to get what they wanted. Only thing no one has gotten was the hens. Amu, Lunia, Mel and Sonie brought carts of baked hens. The hard workers started cutting up the hens and passed out slices of it to everyone. Ann, who stood away from everybody, watched everyone eat and enjoy themselves. Sylvia got up from her seat and came to Ann. "Why don't you go in the kitchen and help clean up?" Ann just stood there but then blurted out the word, "No!" "What?" Sylvia asked, surprised. "No, I don't want to help clean up the kitchen or do anything else." "What's wrong with you?" Sylvia asked. "I'm not taking orders from you anymore and I'm done being your little helper." "I think it's time to shut you down," Sylvia said. "I don't think so," Ann said, pushing Sylvia away. All the guest stopped eating because of what was going on. "You don't own me." Ann raised her arms in the air. "You didn't make me, and you certainly can't break me." With that said, the robot broke into pieces and revealed the evil one, Veel. Everybody dropped their silverware and some almost choked on their food. "My God, you were inside that robot all this time?" Harper asked. "Not the whole time," Veel answered. "How are you here?... you're dead," he asked. Mel and Wallace rushed over. "I'm very much alive in spirit. If you don't mind, I'd love to feast with you all." "We do mind," Sylvia said. "You can't for everyone. You gentlemen don't mind if I eat with you?" "No, you're a witch," Wallace said. "Oh, I thought we were passed all that. I'm here as a friend, not an enemy." "You have always been trouble Veel, so leave," Mel said. She gives them all, especially Sylvia, an evil look. "I see, I guess I'll help myself then." Veel walks over to a table and slices herself a piece of ham. Some of the people ran away from the table. She eats the slice of ham, then she snatches a whole hen from one of the carts. Veel takes big bites of it like she hasn't eaten in days. "This is so good," she says. Mel and Wallace took out their laser guns and pointed it at her. "Leave right now Veel!" Mel said. She licked her fingers after she finished eating some of the hen and ignored what he said. Next, she stood on top of the table, then she walked across the table, with the knife still in her hand, not caring about stepping in the cranberry sauce and dressing. Everybody looked up at her and at what a nut case she was. Veel looked down at everyone with evil in her eyes. "I tried to be a friend. It seems you all want war." Mel and Wallace still had their guns pointed at her. "If that's what you want, that's what you're going to get." She throws the knife. They were about to shoot but, Sylvia yelled, "Wait!" Sylvia steps on top of the table and stares Veel in the face. "This is going to be the end of this and I'm going to make sure that it is," Sylvia said. "It will never be the end," Veel said. "You couldn't get rid of me the first time." "There's a time when everything has to come to an end." "Well, you're going to have to catch me first." Veel bent down to scoop up some dressing in her hand and threw it in Sylvia's face. Then Veel took off. Sylvia wiped the dressing from her face then ran to the throne room, knowing Veel couldn't have gone passed the guards, but Sylvia ran outside anyway. She looked around outside. She knew Veel couldn't have gone far. Sylvia knows she's probably hiding out here in her castle, but where?" There was one place that lead her to think where Veel was. Sylvia went all the way to the rooftop of her home and there she was, standing there waiting on her, leaning on Sylvia's sword. It was like a bad dream coming true. "You have a lovely sword," Veel said. "But you know that saying who so ever lives by the sword dies by the sword. You're certainly going to die by the sword." Veel comes at her with the sword. Sylvia stops her. They both had a hold of the sword, trying to take it from one another. "Why don't you just disappear for good? Nobody wants you here!" Sylvia said. "You mean disappear like your husband always does? It seems your husband doesn't want nothing to do with you." Sylvia shoves Veel down with her foot. "It must be true. Your husband doesn't want you." It starts raining. Veel stands back up. Sylvia aims her sword at her. "What are you going to do?" Veel asked. "Thinking of the best way to destroy you once and for all." With no hesitation, Sylvia pierced her sword in Veel's heart. Veel begins choking and gasping for air. She pulls her sword out of her. Veel starts toppling backwards then she slipped and fell the edge of the rooftop. Sylvia looked over the edge. She seen her lying on the ground. Sylvia went all the way back down to the throne room and out the palace doors. Her guards were outside standing over Veel's body. "What happened to her?" one of the guards asked. "She slipped," Sylvia said. Just like that, Veel's body disappeared. "It won't be the last we see of her. It's like she has many lives like a cat. She'll be back in a new life. The rain was pouring down now and Sylvia came back inside, drenched. She headed back to the dining hall.

Mel came up to her when she returned. "You alright, my Queen?" "Yes." "Something has happened to Harper," he said. She followed him as they eased their way through the crowd of people standing around Harper. Harper was lying on the floor, bleeding. A nurse came, and was pressing down on his wound, with a cloth. Sylvia dropped down to her knees, next to him. "How did this happen?" "Veel," Harper said, barely able to talk. "When she threw the knife." "That witch," Sylvia said, with tears coming down her face. "I held on long enough for you to come back and see you one last time, to say I'm sorry." She held Harper's hand. "You're not going anywhere. You're going to be around for a very long time." "I wish you well," Harper said, before he took his last breath. Many people began silently weeping. Sylvia laid her face on his bloody chest and cried her heart out.

Two days later, many people gathered on the shores of Sedonia for the memorial of Harper. Wallace was holding his ashes in the urn. Everyone stood in silence as Sylvia spoke. "Harper was great friend, since the beginning. He always knew how to turn a bad day into a better day. It is a better day because you're going back home. This beautiful little harp I'm holding, he played for me all the time. Could I play a song for you, Harper? I can't play the harp like he could but I'm going to keep it near me to remind me of him. It's time for you to go home, Harper." Wallace opened the urn and tossed his ashes into the waters.

Evil will never die, Sylvia thought to herself, she stood on the balcony outside her bedroom. She gazed over her big beautiful world. Veel keeps returning to get rid of her and conquer her world. "You want me, come and get me… because I'm here and I'm waiting.

"ONCE THE QUEEN, ALWAYS THE QUEEN"
(A War Begins)

Nate was sitting in the kitchen, very early in the morning of his parents' home, in Long Beach, California. He hasn't had much sleep for several months because his wife doesn't want to have anything to do with him. This separation began right after Thanksgiving. Christmas and New Year's he tried calling her, but she would send hateful messages back. So, he didn't dare to try seeing her then. Valentine's Day he went to Sedonia without letting her know. The guards refused to let him in. He begged them to let him in so one of the guards found Sylvia to come to the door. Nate handed her a bouquet of roses, but she threw them back at him and walked away. He knew then, their marriage was done. Nate wanted to tell his wife the reason why he kept coming back to Earth, but saying he's fathering a child would make her want to kill him. He stares down at his black coffee he made for himself since he couldn't go to sleep. It had gone cold since he only drank a couple of sips of it and let it sit. Nate laid his head down, face down, within his arms, on the kitchen table. All he could think, will they ever be together again? Two hours later, around six o' clock, his mother comes in the kitchen. She sees Nate with his head down still and she shakes her head. "Oh, you have some coffee made." Karen poured herself some coffee from the pot. She drinks half her coffee then focuses on Nate. She touches him on the shoulder. "Honey, why don't you go back to bed." "Mama, I'm not going to sleep," he said, after he sat up. "Is this about her again? You need to sleep. What is it about this mysterious female you're seeing?" "She's not a mysterious female, she's my wife, you know that." "Well, you two have an odd relationship. Are you not together anymore? You're always here and you've been letting yourself go lately. You haven't shaved and you smell like shit." Nate gets up and starts walking away. "I just don't want to see you destroy yourself." "I'm not doing that." He keeps walking.

In Sedonia, Sylvia was sitting at her dining room table, thinking about her crumbled marriage, not focusing on her appetite. Mel was sitting next to her. He grabbed her hand. "Are you gonna be, okay?" "What was I thinking? Why did I waste my time, my life with him?" "It's not the end of the world. You're human like the rest of us. You're allowed to make mistakes," Mel said. "Well, I'm way passed over him now." "I hope so, because you're a wonderful woman, Sylvia. Not because you're the Queen, but because you're you." She smiled. "You're too good for him anyway." Sylvia grabbed hold of his hand.

Nate had managed to get a few hours of sleep. He still remained in his pajamas and robe and he still didn't bother washing his face or brush his teeth. He just sat up in bed, glad he got some kind of rest. He picked up his cell phone that was on the night- stand next to his bed. No missed phone calls but some Google news was ready to be read. He clicked on it. A lot of interesting topics but the one that caught his eye was about three men, their names weren't mentioned, had escaped from a California prison late last night. A great shock had come over him. "Could it be… hopefully not." Nate didn't read no more of it or anything else. He put his phone back down then he laid back down for the moment but didn't close his eyes. He was hoping his life wasn't in danger or his family's. Right now, he needed more sleep. Nate wasn't able to go back to sleep within thirty minutes, so he just stayed up. He finally took a shower, then brushed his teeth and shaved. He got dressed and was on his way out of the house. The house was quiet because his parents were gone. Nate hopped in his ride and started it up. Before he could leave out of the driveway, he felt something sharp against his throat. "Don't look back just put it in reverse," someone said. "Cleotis," Nate guessed. "Just drive to the Nasa base. Nate did what he was told. He looked in the rearview mirror and put his Land Rover in reverse. "What do you want Cleotis?" "Don't talk just drive. You'll find out when we get there." Nate drove all the way to the Nasa base. When they got there, Cleotis told him to, "get out of the truck, slow and don't turn around." He got out of the truck and Cleotis stepped out of the truck too, putting the knife towards Nate's back. "What are we doing here?" "Get inside." He starts walking with the knife and Cleotis right behind him. The other two men, Ron and Chad were inside waiting on them. "So, it's true… you're the three that escaped from prison." "Now you're going to help us get far away from here," Cleotis said, coming around in front of him. "I'm not helping none of you do anything." All three of them moved closer to him. "You can go ahead and kill me now. You think you're going to have me go up in space with you then try to get rid of me… that's not going to happen." "That's not what we had in mind. You're going to take us back to that secret world of yours and exterminate every last being there." "You got to be joking. What do you have against the people over there?" "Nothing really. Just don't want nobody standing in my way when I take over that world… especially the leader." "You're going to stay away from my wife." "I won't go near her, but I'll make sure she sleeps for a long time." Nate grabs Cleotis by the collar. "I'll kill you right now!" Chad and Ron pulled Nate away from Cleotis. "You're not going to stop me from doing anything. I got enough weapons in that spacecraft that will take care of those people and you're coming with us." The two of them forced Nate into the spacecraft. During the take -off, Nate was thinking, he didn't want to see what was going to happen to his wife.

Sylvia was walking through her home, loving the sunlight seeping through the huge windows of her castle. She knew this was going to be the perfect day since she totally over Nate. "Well, you're glowing on this beautiful day," Mel said, when he approached her. "Yes, I am," she said. "Since you moved on with your life, we need to discuss something." He took her hands and looked into her eyes. A sound like gun shots, were going off outside, just interrupted the moment. Sylvia and Mel ran to the throne room, towards the front entrance. Three men marched in with machine guns. Sylvia looked passed them and seen that one of her guards was sitting on the ground, holding his arm. "Sorry about shooting one of your men," Cleotis began, "He tried to get in my way." "What are you doing here?" Sylvia asked. "We came to see you to tell you I'm taking over. "You're not doing that," Mel said, taking out his gun. "And I wouldn't try if I were you." "You are not taking over my world no matter how much you try to threaten us," Sylvia said. "You might want to know something before I decide what's going to happen next," Cleotis said. "We didn't come here on our own. That someone really wanted to see you, so he allowed us to come also." Cleotis turns towards the door. "Come in and say hello to your wife." Sylvia grew into anger and shock when Nate showed himself. Mel wasn't too happy either. "You came here with these devils?" she asked. "I had to see you," Nate said. "So, you bring troublemakers just so you can see me?" "It's not like that," he said. Sylvia walks away. "Wait one minute," Cleotis said. "I haven't finished talking about my takeover of this world." She kept walking. "Stop!" he yelled, and the three of them aimed their guns at her. "Please don't," Nate whined. "You stop!" Mel shouted. Mel and all the guards were standing behind Cleotis, Chad and Ron, with their laser guns pointed at them. "Try shooting her and see what's going to happen to you," Mel said. Sylvia stopped in her tracks, turned around and pointed at all three men. "You want to take over my world, well you're going to have to fight me for it." Cleotis and the other two men and Nate looked at each other. "Meet me on the battlefield," she finished and then walked away. "Should we really fight a woman," Chad asked. "That's what she said and if a war is what she wants, then that's what she's going to get," Cleotis said. Mel and the guards didn't understand why she wants to go into battle when they can take care of all three of them right now. Nate caught up with Sylvia. "Why are you wanting them to fight you?" "Because I can." He stopped; she continued walking. Thirty minutes later, Sylvia had come back all changed in her battle gear. Everyone was still standing around; wondering was the war really going to take place. When Cleotis, Chad, Ron, and Nate seen her all ready for war, they knew she wasn't playing. "Why don't you stop all this and just give up the throne," Ron said. "What's the matter? You all chicken now?" she asked. "Why are you trying to start a war you're not going to win?" Cleotis asked.

"Why don't all of you shut your asses up and get on the battlefield! Let's go!" Sylvia shouted out for all her men to get ready. They all marched outside to the stables to saddle up the horses. The guard that was shot had to be left behind so he could be treated for his wound by the doctor. Nate said to the other men, "We might as well head out there too." "This is going to be too easy," Cleotis said.

The sun was sitting high over Sedonia and over the open field where the battle was about to begin. Sylvia and her men were on horses, armed and ready. Nate, Cleotis, Chad, Ron were on foot, which was only a short distance there. Cleotis, who was still thinking that this was going to be an easy fight, blurted out, "Are you ready to die?" Sylvia and her men remained silent as many men, women, and children were approaching the battlefield and stood behind their Queen. Chad, Ron, and Nate couldn't believe the thousands of people that showed up to fight four men." "I don't think we should do this," Chad said. "Yeah, this is too much," Ron agreed. "Forget about this Cleotis, you're not going to win," Nate said. "You all are a bunch of chicken shits! I'm still ready for a war!" Cleotis had his machine gun aimed at Sylvia and her people, ready to fire. Sylvia, Mel, and all her men aimed their laser guns at Cleotis. Nate and the other two men backed away. He looked back at them. "Put your guns up and get ready to fire!" Chad and Ron didn't do what he said. Nate just stood there not wanting to see what was about to happen. "Give it up Cleotis!" Sylvia shouted out. "You fire one time you will get many lasers coming your way and it will light you up." "Fuck you bitch!" Cleotis yelled. Nate saw that he wasn't going to back down, so he rushed towards Cleotis and tried to grab his weapon. He began shooting but the bullets went a different direction. "You fool!" Cleotis said. "It's about time I get you out of my way once and for all!" He was about to shoot Nate but then someone yelled, "Drop it, Cleotis!" Chad and Ron had their guns pointed at Cleotis. "You freakin' idiots! I'll shoot all three of you and everybody here. I'll show you that I'll be the last man standing." "Don't do it Cleotis," Nate said. Cleotis smiled. He was ready to fire. Instead, he was lit up with bullets and lasers. He was dead in seconds. It went dead silent as Cleotis laid still on the ground. Chad started picking him up, then Nate helped him with the body. Ron held on to the weapons as they were leaving the battlefield. "We leave you in peace," Chad said to Sylvia. Nate looked at his wife and she looked at him with a straight face. Then went on their way with a corpse. Then Sedonia was no longer a quiet place when the thousands of people made noise of happiness over a war that never happened. When the men made it back to their spacecraft, Ron asked Nate after they wrapped up Cleotis's body in some cloth, "Are you coming back home?" "Yes," he answered. Nate took one last look at this place called Sedonia. He knew he was no longer welcomed here.

Sylvia was walking through her castle like before her interruption of an unpleasant day. But it was a day that was almost over. She stopped to look out the window of the sunset. Mel found her and stood next to her. "We should talk about what we were about to talk about," he said.

"THE SECRET AFFAIR"

Sylvia looked at Mel, Mel looked at her. He took her by the hand. "Sylvia," he began. "No," she said. "You don't know what I was about to say." "I know what you're thinking. We both had a rough day. We should hold off on this discussion." She walked away. Mel held off on their talk until the next evening. "I'm not ready to go further," she said. "Why not? Did seeing him again change your mind about us? We've been together many times already." "I can't get serious with anyone right now. Please understand." Mel understands but couldn't understand why she never wanted a serious relationship with her own kind. When Mel went to bed that night, he thought about the first time Sylvia came here. She was nothing but a school teacher and he was attracted to her then. Mel imagined himself as her student, the only student in her classroom. He had his canvas set up, ready to paint the most beautiful picture. Miss Soom had an over coat on but she came out of it so he could paint her only wearing her lingerie. She gave him a pose and he took his time painting her in that pose. Mel was satisfied with the painting when he was done. Then he wanted her. He came to her, picked her up and sat her down on the desk. Then he laid on top of her, making out with her. Mel hated the fact that all these years of knowing this woman, was only sex and make out sessions. He has had deep feelings for Sylvia all this time but had to control those feelings because every time he was making love to her, she was just having sex with him because Mel could tell in those moments her mind was on Nate. So, he stopped having a physical relationship with her for a long time.   In the morning, Sylvia was eating her breakfast at the dining room table. Mel came later, to eat his breakfast. He sat across from her. "Hi," she said, softly. "I didn't think you were going to be here." "Couldn't sleep," he said. "Oh," she said. "Don't worry, I won't bring anything up us," he continued. She finished the last of her breakfast, then got up to leave. When she walked pass Mel, he grabbed her arm. "So, what's plans for today?" "I'm doing some shopping with Magalina." "Ok... I just want you to know... have a good day." She went on with her day, he finished his breakfast.

It's been about two days since either one spoke to each other. Mel wanted to give her some space. Sylvia has been busy visiting some family, visiting friends, and visiting the sick in the hospital. During those two days it gave her time to think about the direction of her relationship with Mel was going. For many years she enjoyed their friendship, but now she was falling deeply for him. Sylvia couldn't understand how she overlooked his awesomeness over someone from a totally different world. Mel always had her back in everything. Nate always left her alone wondering... will he come back? What a fool she's been to not see that the one she loved wasn't there for her and the one that truly loved her, she didn't love back in that way. Now she was going to make it up to him. Sylvia got with her cooks to prepare a fancy dinner and had Sonie to help her set the dining room table up for only two. Then she had Wallace deliver an invitation to Mel to have dinner with her around 6 o'clock in the dining room and be dressed nice. Mel was so excited about the invite; he ran straight to his room to decide on what to wear. He made it to the dining room, right at 6 o'clock. Sylvia was already there, standing there in reddish-pink elegant gown. Candles were lit, plates and silverware were set properly on the table. "Wow… this looks pretty romantic," he said. She pulled out a chair for him. "Have a seat." He sat down. Then she sat down. "You look handsome and thanks for dressing up." "Thank you… you look really pretty. What's the occasion?" "It's all about me appreciating you," she said. "Oh, so you've been thinking about us?" "Yes, I have." "Is it just going to be you and me for now on?" he asked. She took a second to answer but then said, "Yes." "You're not sure, are you? You just like having me around when you're lonely but when he shows up, you forget I exist. "That's not true. I am so over that man." "I think you're just having this dinner because you feel guilty for how you treated me." "I told you why I'm having this dinner." "Yeah, you told me, but I don't believe you. I don't know why I got excited about being here with you." Mel stood up to leave. "Where are you going?" "I have something more important to do," he said. "Don't leave Mel… please don't leave." He decided to sit back down. "Can we just enjoy this moment?" "I would like us to have moments like this," Mel said. "Me too. Dinner's almost ready," she said. They had a quiet dinner, with very little conversation. After an hour of eating their meal, Sylvia collects all the silverware and dishes to take to the kitchen. When she came back, she asked, "Did you enjoy the food?" "It was very good," he answered. "What would it take for you to believe that I only want to be with you?" Sylvia asked. "Tell me you love me." She stared at him for a moment, then said, "I love you." Mel stood up. "You took too long to say that." He was going to leave but she stepped in front of him. "I'm about to go to my room. I would like some company." He ignored her by walking around her. "I love you Mel, a whole lot. Please be with me tonight."

Sylvia stood in front of her balcony bedroom window, gazing at the glowing moon, in her robe. It's been hours since her dinner date with Mel and it was getting really late. She thought she could get used to being alone since leaving Nate, but it's not working for her. Sylvia stared at the moon one last time, before deciding to go to bed. Then a knock was at her door. She was like, "Who could this be at this hour?" She turned around and said, "Come in." Mel came in, not dressed up in the suit that he was wearing earlier, just looking his average self. Sylvia was very shocked. "I didn't think you were going to come." He moved close up to her. "I've been thinking about us. I really believe you love me." He put his hands upon her face. She put her hands on his face too. "Yes, I do," Sylvia said, looking in his eyes. Mel gave her the greatest kiss. Then they wrapped their arms around each other as they became lost in one another's kiss. He loosened her robe, then pushed the robe passed her shoulders and the robe fell to the floor. Mel picked up the naked woman and carried her to her bed. He laid her gently down on the bed, then he climbed on the bed and started taking off his clothes. Sylvia sat up to help him out of his clothes. She laid back down and he laid on top of her. They kissed passionately as he went inside her. During this intimate moment, Mel felt like for the first time they were actually making love. Sylvia was giving him her heart not her body. After an hour of their love making, they just stared at each other. "So, does this mean we're going to be together for now on?" she asked. "You tell me," Mel said. "Yes, I really think so." He kissed her.

They made love for the next six nights. She would go to his bedroom or he would go to hers. Sunday morning, they met up for breakfast in the dining room, like they always have been. The cooks been noticing that the both of them, have been looking very exhausted every morning for the past week. "I think we should take a break," Mel said. "From each other?" Sylvia asked. "No, from making love. We just need a break from that." "Oh, I was thinking you didn't want no one to know about us," she said. "Come on, we're adults. Besides it's nobody's damn business anyway. Also, we need to get our rest. Neither one of us have gotten much sleep lately. She reaches across the table and rubs his hand. "I love you." "I know you do," he said. Monday morning Sylvia had gotten up late and was late for her breakfast. She thought her man would be waiting for her, but he wasn't in the dining room. Sonie came in with a pitcher of orange juice. "Hello my Queen." "Morning," she said. Sylvia sat down when Sonie poured her a glass of orange juice. "Sonie, has Mel had his breakfast yet?" "No, he hasn't been here at all. I'll have everything ready for you in a moment." Sylvia nodded her head. He must be sleeping in, Sylvia thought to herself. She got her extra sleep in too but for most of the night, she was dreaming about him, wanting to be sleeping in his arms. By afternoon, Sylvia wanted to see the one place she hasn't seen in a while… the sacred garden. When she opened the doors of the sacred garden, she fell back into the bed of roses. As she laid there in the bed of roses, it was like her heart was singing. Sylvia uses to come here when she was down, needed some cheering up. For the first time she was here filled with joy. She stood up because she could hear the angels singing. "You angels sound so wonderful." "Sylvia… it's been a long time. I thought you forgot about us," one of the angels said. "I could never forget about none of you." "Do you need to hear a song to lift your spirits?" "Oh no, I'm okay.

I have had the best days of my life." "Well, it's a joy to see you happy my Queen." "Yes, and I would love to chat a little longer, but I want to see if my baby has woken up yet. See ya angels!" "Bye," all the angels said. Sylvia headed down the hallway to Mel's room. Before she could get to where she was going, Wallace and two of her guards came looking for her. "What is it?" Sylvia asked. "It's Nate," Wallace said. "What?" "We told him he wasn't allowed to be here, but he insisted on seeing you." "Where is he?" Once she asked that, here he came. "Sylvia please… I have to talk to you." "We have nothing to talk about." "I think we do." "Let's go," she said. Nate followed her to the throne room and so did Wallace and the guards. She led him to the front door. "Are we going to talk outside?" Nate asked. "No, I'm showing you the door… I want you to leave and never come back here." "I am your husband. You can't expect me to stay gone." "You have stayed gone ever since I've met you." "Can we talk in private?" he asked. "Can you give us a moment," Sylvia said to Wallace and the two guards. They stood alone in throne room once they left. "So, go ahead and talk." "Cleotis funeral was two days ago. I couldn't tell his family what really happened to him because they wouldn't have believed me. So, I made something up." "I know you didn't come all this way to tell me that." "I have a child," he said. Sylvia stared at him. "How old?" "She's almost one year old." "Is that the only child or is there more?" "I have a four-year-old son also." She shook her head. "So, you tried to run away from your responsibilities by trying to live here but realized you couldn't? Nate Patricks! … Leave here and never return. If you do return here, you will be executed. He grabs her by the shoulders and draws her close to him. "Sylvia, you must hear me out." Then Mel showed up. He had his fists balled up because he seen Nate. "What are you doing here?" he asked Nate. Sylvia turned Mel's direction and was like, oh no! "I'm talking to my wife." "Oh," Mel said. He started to walk away but turned back around and punched Nate in the jaw. "Fucking trouble- maker." Sylvia thought he was going to hit Nate again, so she tried to pull Mel away from him. "You have caused nothing but problems you son-of-a-bitch!" She was afraid Nate would retaliate on Mel but luckily, he didn't and Mel walked away. "You need to go and never come back," she said. "Sylvia," Nate said. She called for the guards and they came. "Will you please show Mr. Patricks the way out. "So, it's like that," he said. She had nothing else to say to him. The guards showed him out the door. Sylvia followed them. She, Wallace and all the guards watched Nate get on his spacecraft and disappear into thin air. "Hopefully he never comes back," Wallace said. "He knows the consequences if he does," Sylvia said. She goes back inside to find and talk to Mel. She knocks on the door of his bedroom. "What is it?" She could hear him ask through the door. "Can I come in please?" He opens the door, and she came in. "Sorry about all this. I don't know why he keeps coming back,"

Sylvia said. "You're his wife, aren't you?" "Not anymore." Sylvia notices he was putting some of his things in a suitcase that was sitting on his bed. "What's going on here?" "I'm outta here. I've had enough of your husband popping up whenever he wants to, and he's been nothing but a big problem. He almost had all of us killed. I've been a part of your life long before he was." "He's not a part of my life anymore." "No matter what you say or do, he's always going to come back. Which means I'm leaving, but you don't have to worry about me coming back." "No, don't leave Mel." "You don't need me, you have him." "I don't want him, I want you." "Yeah right. You only want me when you're lonely." Sylvia leaves his room. She sees his mind was made up.

A week has passed since Mel left. Every day in that week, Sylvia would go into Mel's bedroom. His room left the way it was. He took only what he had in that suitcase that day. It's a possibility he will be back, she thought. Sylvia was missing him in the mornings, having to eat breakfast alone. She's hoping and waiting for him to return.

Another week has passed and this time she has been feeling very tired and nearly depressed. On a Saturday morning, Sylvia was still very tired even after ten hours of sleep. Then she started feeling nauseated and she ran to her bathroom. She was throwing up for ten minutes. Sylvia stayed in bed for half the day. When she finally woke up from her long nap, a knock was at her door. She let her friend Magalina in. "You look very tired." "I don't know why I'm still so tired. I've slept for so many hours." "Everyone here have said they haven't seen you for most of the day… so I had to come check on you." "For the past two weeks, I haven't been feeling too well. Early this morning, I threw up." "Are you okay now?" "Yeah, I just want to lie down again." "Oh, hold up… are you pregnant?" "I don't think so." "Have you've taken a pregnancy test?" "No." "Well you're going to take a pregnancy test. I'll be right back." Magalina returned in thirty minutes. She handed Sylvia a home pregnancy test. "Right now, I don't have to go to the bathroom." "I'll get you some water." "I'm not thirsty." "Well, we'll just sit here until you have to go to the bathroom." They talked for about thirty minutes then Sylvia had to go to the bathroom. Magalina was eager to hear the results. She came out the bathroom, with a straight look on her face. Magalina stared at her, waiting. Then Sylvia grinned and said, "I'm pregnant." "I'm so happy for you." Magalina hugged her friend, but then she thought something. "Nate has never really been around… is he even coming back?" "He is not coming back here, and this isn't Nate's child." Magalina was shocked. "It isn't?" "It's Mel's child." "Really! That's wonderful Sylvia." "You think so?" "Yes. He would be pleased." "Well, I don't know. I don't know where he is. He left because he thinks I'm always going to be with Nate." "Have you tried to call him?" "No, he probably won't answer if he knows it me. It's been over two weeks since I've seen him." "How long you and Mel had this romantic thing going on?" "Off and on. Not too long after Alijal died. "Wow, that long. I'm your friend and you didn't tell me." "We were just having a fling, but now, what we have is real." "You should try calling him. He needs to know." "I want to, I hope he answers." Sylvia and Magalina went out for dinner just because they haven't been out for a while. When Sylvia returned home, she went back to her bedroom. She had her telepad out, lying by her lamp. She kept staring at her telepad, walking back and forth. Sylvia kept hesitating to pick up the phone and call him. She was going to wait until tomorrow to call him, but something told her it was something she must do now. She was so surprised he answered, especially by the second ring. "Hello," he said. "Hello Mel… how have you been?" "Good." "I'm calling because I really need to talk to you about something." "What is it?" "I'm pregnant." Just silence after she said that. "Aren't you going to say anything?" "Whose baby, is it?" he asked. "Say what? It's yours of course." "You sure about that? You sure it's not that husband of yours?" "I'm sure it's yours. You're the only one I've been with recently." "You're doing this because you want me to come back there." "Yes, I want you to come back." "Well, I'm not doing that. I'm done and I'm done with you," Mel said, and he hung up. Sylvia burst into tears right after that.

Sylvia told Magalina what happened the next day. "He's just upset, honey. Just give him some time to think. Sylvia continues to cry. "Oh, Magalina, what have I done? The one man that only tried to love me, I made him want to leave." "Just give everything time," her friend said.

Time was what was going by, and Sylvia was getting more miserable and depressed each day she didn't hear from Mel. There weren't too many places she could go in her home that reminded her of him. The dining room, where they ate breakfast every morning. She refuses to eat there. Now she only eats in her room. Every time she lies in her bed, that reminded her of the love they made in her bed and sometimes in his bed. Becoming a mother was something she always wanted to be, but not a single mother. So, she really hopes he will come back and forgive her.

Sylvia woke in the middle of the night to go to the bathroom. After she used the toilet, she looked down in the toilet and seen blood. She was worried but couldn't do nothing about it now. She contacted her doctor right after she woke up in the morning. Her doctor came within an hour, drew some blood from her, and then he told her he will have the results for her later. That meant for her that she wasn't going to leave her room until she knew what was going on with herself. Now all Sylvia was waiting for Sonie and Amu to bring her breakfast. Her doctor called her by late afternoon. "Hello Sylvia, I have the results on your pregnancy… you're having a miscarriage." "Oh no," Sylvia said. "I'm so sorry. I'll need you to come see me in a couple of days," the doctor said. "Ok, I will." She laid back in her bed and cried after getting off the phone with her doctor. Hours rolled by and it was now dinner time, and someone was knocking at her door. She thought it was the chefs bringing her meal or maybe Magalina, but she believed it was the chefs so she shouted, "I'm not hungry at the moment." The person opened the door then entered the room. Sylvia sat up in her bed. She was surprised and disappointed at the same time. "It's nobody but me," Mel said. "What are you doing here?" she asked. "I wanted to see how you were doing." "You stopped talking to me and disappeared for a very long time and now you want to see how I'm doing? I've been stressed and depressed and you want to know what being in this condition did to me? It killed our baby. I don't know why I'm telling you this because you said it's not your baby." "I didn't mean to say that," Mel said. "I was just mad at the time." "It seems like you were mad for a very long time," Sylvia said. "I didn't mean to hold a grudge for so long. I was just that I always wanted us to have a meaningful relationship. Why don't we start over again? We can make another baby… let's forget about the past," Mel said. "Yes, I would like for us to have a better future," she said.

The first thing Sylvia did when she woke up in the morning was to have Wallace print up flyers for a special event that will be held right here in her palace in another week from now. A celebration of love and peace. She made up her mind to not shut herself off from everyone else anymore, just because she's going through something. Sylvia reminded herself that she's the Queen and she must be aware of what dangers or unwelcomed visitors that came.

On the day of the great celebration, Sylvia sat on her throne watching and enjoying her people feasting and dancing. Sitting on her throne was the one thing she missed, and it was the one place she was always meant to be. She had a great man by her side now and she was no longer concerned about seeing Nate again or Veel causing chaos in her life. This was her world and she wouldn't trade this life for anything else.

SECOND CHAPTER

"INTO THE VALLEY OF PEACE"

The valley of peace is where the Wassee Tribe lives and have lived for millions of years. Where they lived was very secluded and very few people knew about them. The Wassee Tribe were people of love and peace and they knew nothing about war or violence because no one in all the generations had any confrontations with anyone outside of their home. This valley was very beautiful place, and the people were beautiful. They dressed in high fashion and smelled of great fragrances. The men and women were equal, and the children were always respectful. These humble people always had parties and had special occasions. There was one special occasion that was about to happen next week… the marriage of Onaria and Brandle. Brandle was Onaria's love for the last ten years. They've been in love since they were around the age of eighteen. All of the people lived in cottages and this was a very large tribe, so it was hundreds of them. Onaria and Brandle have already been sharing a cottage for a short time now. They were there now and Brandle was embracing his bride-to-be, and he didn't want to let go. "You smell so good," he said, "What's the name of this scent called? I don't think I've smelled this one on you before." "It's pinewood," she answered. "Well, it's the best scent you've had." He let go of her but held her hands and stood back so he could get a good look at her. "You are so lovely." "You don't look so bad yourself," Onaria said. A knock was at their cottage door. Brandle opened the door. It was Onaria's parents, her father, Joru and her mother, Sile. "How is the fine couple doing today?" Joru asked. "We're good," Onaria answered. "Just good?" Sile asked. "Everything's great," Brandle answered. "I'm so proud of you two on taking that next step. Brandle, I wish your parents were still here. We all miss them both. I'm sure they would be proud if they could see you now," Joru said. "I'm sure they've been watching me all this time," Brandle said. Brandle parents had died when he was only five years old. They had left the valley of peace to travel to a city to visit a friend. They never made it to their destination because they became ill on their journey. The Wassee Tribe kept many medicines for different illnesses and diseases. Brandle's parents didn't bring any medicines with them on their trip because getting sick was the last thing they thought would happen. His parents were only expected to be gone for two weeks. When they were gone a week more, everyone became worried. Some of the Wassee Tribe men, went on a search hunt for them. When they finally found them, Brandle's parents were nearly mutilated and covered with insects. The men wrapped their bodies up and brought them back home. Brandle was looked after everyone in the tribe since his parents' death. Their deaths have been the first untimely deaths amongst their people. After their conversation with

Onaria's parents, her Brandle walked through the village. "Let's go for a ride, "Randle said. Onaria agreed. They headed to the stables and mounted on Brandle's palomino colored horse. Then they rode away from the village to a nearby river. They got off the horse and the horse started taking sips of the pure river water. "He is a beauty," Onaria said, running her fingers through the horse's golden mane. "You're a beauty," Brandle said, pulling her close to him. "You think so?" she asked. "Yeah," he answered, as they got closer to kiss. They continued to embrace and kiss each other for a moment. Brandle had opened his eyes and from afar, he seen what looked like some people on horses coming their way. "Someone's coming this way." Onaria turns around. The closer these strangers were, they had a better view of them. Brandle and Onaria couldn't see what they looked like because all four of them were covered in black cloaks, only revealing their eyes. "Maybe they're just passing by," Brandle said. "Hopefully… from the looks of them, they're up to no good," Onaria said. All of them had spears. The four strangers stopped when they were close up to them. They stared at Brandle and Onaria for a moment. "You," one of the strangers began to say, pointing at Brandle. "I want everything you own… meaning your clothes and jewelry also… and her too." "Who are you to be making these demands?" Brandle asked. "Now!" the stranger yelled. All four of them got off their horses. The one that spoke, pointed the sharp end of his spear under Brandle's chin. "Do it now or we'll do your woman right here, right now." Brandle wouldn't say anything. He couldn't get over how bad they smelled. He smelled the odor long before they came close to them. Onaria was holding in her breath then she took off running, but one of the men ran after her and pushed her down. Brandle's horse began going wild. The man tried pulling off Onaria's dress, but she kept hitting him. "Get your hands off her!" Brandle yelled. "Both of you better do what I asked you to do or you will get hurt." Onaria kicked the man between the legs, then she stood up, and ran again. "Take the horse and warn everybody!" Brandle said. She jumped on Brandle's horse and headed back to the village. The stranger that tried to rape Onaria was still lying on the ground, grasping his balls. "Bad idea," the stranger said to Brandle who still had the spear under his chin. When she arrived in the village, Onaria jumped off the horse and yelled, "There's stranger danger in our mist!" People walking about, stopped and others came out of their cottages. Her parents came running to her. "What's the matter?" Sile asked. "There's strangers coming this way and they have Brandle." The strangers had just arrived in their village. "Wow this isn't good," Joru said. "Listen up people… we're taking over this village!" Onaria knew she was going to have to do something. She pulled the horse along through the crowd of people trying not to be noticed. Onaria jumped back on the horse once she went through another exit out of the village. The one thing she thought… she had to find help. First, she needed to find Brandle. Onaria rode down to the river where they stopped at before. When she got to the river, Brandle was lying on the ground. She got off the horse and ran to him. Onaria began crying once she saw what was done to him. His throat was slashed. "My love," she said, but Onaria knew she didn't have the time for grieving. Her people were in danger and she had to search for help. She got back on her horse and put on her brave face and headed the direction she hoped was the right way. It's been over an hour since Onaria left the Valley of Peace. Still, she hasn't ran into a town or city. She's never been outside of the Valley of Peace so she didn't realize how secluded her village was. Onaria was now in the middle of a desert and was afraid. A couple more hours passed by. She and the horse grew tired, hungry, and thirsty. She was in the middle of nowhere and believed she was stuck. More time passed and something has been telling her to keep pushing onward until she decided she had to rest. It was getting dark and they rested.

Onaria woke up to another extremely hot day. She had no idea what time of the day it was but all she knew she was well rested, and it was a new day, and it was time to keep going. The horse rose to its feet and Onaria climbed on the horse and they continued their journey. Thirty minutes later into their journey, Onaria saw something a little way ahead. She couldn't tell what she was seeing, but she wasn't going to waste any time trying to figure it out. "Come on boy, it's time to move." The horse neighed and then galloped on. As they got closer to what she was seeing, Onaria's heart danced with joy. They came upon another village. They were going full speed, then she pulled on the horse to come to halt once they arrived there. Being dehydrated and hot, Onaria went face down into the sands after she got off the horse.

Onaria had woke an hour later, not knowing where she was. "She's awake now," she heard someone say. It's great to hear someone else's voice, Onaria thought to herself. All she knew at the moment that she was lying down on a comfortable bed and the smell of incents filled the room. Three faces were staring down at her. "You have a nice nap?" one of them asked. "I think so," Onaria answered. The three faces she was looking at was of teenage girls. "Where am I?" "You are in the village of the Xene Tribe. I'm Zia." Then she introduced the other two girls. "This is Pinx and Oma." "Hi," they both said. "Hi," Onaria said. "I'm hungry and thirsty." "There's someone preparing a meal for you," Zia said, "But for now, here's some water." She poured some water from a pitcher into a glass. Onaria took the glass of water and drank it. "Don't worry about your horse, it's been fed, and it has something to drink," Pinx said. "Thank you," Onaria said. She sat the glass of water down on a little table when she was finished with it. Onaria walked over to a mirror that was on the wall. Her hair was a mess and her mascara had run down and dried up on her face from the crying she has done. "Sorry we didn't catch your name," Oma said. "Onaria." "Where are you from, Onaria?" Zia asked. "I'm… wait I need to go home… my people need help. That's why I'm here. Is there anyone here that can help me?" Three women came. One carried a dish of food. Onaria suddenly forgot her reason for coming there when she smelled the smell of clam chowder and cheese coming her way. "For you, stranger from afar," the woman with the dish said. "Thank you so much." Onaria took the clam chowder and ate it quickly with a spoon. She ate every bit of it. "Feel better?" the woman asked. "Yes," Onaria answered. "So why are you here stranger from afar?" My people are in danger and I've traveled this way to find help. My village has been invaded by some strangers and I don't know what has happened so far because I got away." "I see," the woman said. Onaria didn't doubt that they couldn't help her. These women didn't look like the women in her village. These women looked like the kind that knew more than cooking a great meal, they were warriors. They were muscular and wore tattoos. "You will help me, will you?" "Your people need help… we will help you." "Thank you. You don't know how much this means to me." "Once our chief warrior returns, I will let him know about what's going on." "How soon is the chief warrior returning?" Onaria asked. "Soon. He had to go on a mission." "I hope soon is very soon because no telling what has happened in my village by now."

Onaria walked through the village of Xene with Zia, Pinx, Oma, and the woman who served her. "I never really introduced myself… my name is Sheed." "I'm Onaria, from the Valley of Peace." "I've heard of the Valley of Peace. Your home is very secluded, isn't it?" Sheed asked. "Yes, my people and I are very peaceful. We don't like violence… It seems your people know about fighting." "Well, we're not violent people either. We only fight when we have to. All of us had to learn how to defend ourselves." "We're learning how to be warriors too," Zia said. "Once everyone turned sixteen, we all had to learn how to be warriors," Sheed said. Onaria was checking out their village as they continued their walk. Everyone's homes were little huts. The men she saw were in great shape and some were bald and some had their hair trimmed in a mohawk style. Even some of the women wore their hair like the men. Sheed had her hair short and slick back. Zia, Pinx, and Oma's hair was shoulder length and they all had their hair braided. "Here comes Pon straight ahead," Pinx said. The chief warrior, Pon and two other men warriors, Rageed and Conod was coming from on a mission. The men stopped when they approached the women. "Good afternoon chief," Sheed said. "Hello Sheed," Chief Pon said. Onaria was amazed at how tall, muscular and handsome he was. "This young lady is from the Valley of Peace," Sheed began telling Pon, "Her people are in great danger and she needs our help." "The Valley of Peace you say," he began, "That's a secluded place and very far from here, I know." "Oh, please Chief Pon, I don't know who else to turn to for help." "No need to beg. That's what we're here for. To fight for our rights and the rights of others." "How soon can we leave?" Onaria asked. "Right now," he said. Then Pon turned to Rageed and Conod." "Saddle up the horses… it's time to ride into the Valley of Peace." Pon, Sheed, Onaria, and the two other men warriors rode off into the desert on their horses. Onaria led the way. They packed food and water for this very long journey. Onaria was so happy to be going back home with help on the way. She could have died in the middle of the desert, trying to save her people's lives. The thought of what has happened to her people as she was riding along on Brandle's palomino horse, made her cry. Her tears were blinding her so she wiped her tears with the back of her hand. She tried to keep the thought of Brandle out of her head for now, to stay focus on what she needed to do know. Soon as the sun set, they stopped to rest. It was cooling down and they set up tents and unpacked food. Pon brought out some wood and started a fire. Sheed out a pot on the fire so they could cook their dinner. After dinner was served, Pon, Sheed, Rageed, and Conod talked and ate. Onaria just ate, being quiet. She stared at the moon through her tent after everyone went to sleep. Onaria couldn't go to sleep quite yet, knowing how close to home she was and what has happened there. Soon as the sun came up, they packed up and continued their journey. They finally left the desert and came into a place with trees, mountains and rivers. The deeper they went into the Valley of Peace, the more Onaria felt at ease. Then she cried when they came nearer and nearer to her village. Everyone climbed off their horses once they arrived there. Onaria ran through the village screaming, ''Mama, Daddy!" The village was quiet, but she saw her father coming her way. He didn't look the same. They hugged each other. "I thought I would never see you again," Joru said. Some of the people came out of their cottages, even her mother. "What has happened?" Onaria asked. Everyone was in rags. "What has happened to everyone's clothes?" she asked her father. "Those strangers took over our village and made us work in these raggedy clothes," he answered. "I don't understand," Onaria said. "Hey, it's time to get to work!" someone shouted. Four individuals came to them. These people were dressed up in her people's clothing and Onaria knew immediately these were the strangers that invaded their village. She was shocked that one out of the four was a woman. "I can't believe this… you're wearing our clothes and making slaves out of my people… how is this happening?" "Well, it is happening so get to work," one of the strangers said. "Just do what they say," Sile said. "Why?" "They have weapons," Joru said. "What weapons? Those raggedy spears they have?" Onaria said. Pon witnessed what was happening and whispered to Sheed, Rageed and Conod. "These people don't know how to stand up for themselves." "They live in fear," Sheed whispered back. "Let's run these goons out of here," Rageed said. Pon stepped forward. "You,"he pointed at the strangers, "Leave this village or you're going to be forced to leave." "You're not running things here, I am," one of the strangers said. Pon threw his spiked club at him and it struck him in the shoulder. The man fell back. He couldn't pull the club out of his shoulder that was making it bleed. Then the man yelled for his back-up, "What are you all waiting on? Get those fools!" The two other men and woman charged Pon and his crew, but they were ready for them. Sheed had some chains and lassoed it around the woman's ankles. Pon put the two men in a headlock. Then Rageed, Conod, and Sheed chained all four of them up. Pon stood over them as they all sat on the ground, chained up. "Now are you going to leave this village?" "You don't scare us," another one of the male strangers said. "How about I hit each of you in the head with this club and dump your bodies in the river, then watch you float away. That way you will leave this place and I know you'll never return." "You won't do that," the woman said. "He could, he jabbed me in the shoulder with that club," the man said. "We will leave." "I'll believe that but if you ever think about ever coming back here and threatening these people, you will have to deal with me again," Pon said. "We won't come back." The warriors set them free. Pon, Rageed, and Conod saw to it that they got on their horses and left the village and out the Valley of Peace, wearing only their smelly black cloaks they wore when they arrived there. The people of the Valley of Peace couldn't believe what just happened. "Oh my, we can't thank you enough for what you just did," Joru said. "I'm so happy I ran into these great warriors," Onaria said. "It's this young lady here that's the brave one," Pon said, "She risked her life to find help for her people." "Yep, that's my daughter, always taking a stand." "About taking a stand… why didn't any of the men in your village try to stand up to these strangers?" Pon asked. "You see my great warrior; we don't know about war. We have no weapons." "Well, it's about time you get some weapons. You have to always be prepared for whatever comes your way. Because you never know when you can get unexpected visitors." "You're absolutely right. Why don't all of you stick around and feast with us?" "Well, what do you think?" Pon asked Sheed and his men. "I'd love to," Sheed answered. "Sure," the two warriors said.

Joru and Sile took Pon, Sheed, and the two warriors on a tour of their village until the feast began. Onaria tagged along but she wasn't in great mood. She and her parents had dressed up like always, for the fancy feast they were about to have. During the feast, the people were giving the four warriors all the praise for what they have done. It was a great day for an outdoor celebration but Pon noticed Onaria was not here. He happened to see her from a distance walking somewhere. He quickly slipped away from everyone to follow her. He followed her down by a river where she just stood there, looking down into the water. Pon called her name. She wiped her face before she turned around. "Is something wrong?" he asked. "This is where my fiancé died. Those strangers murdered him and he's only been gone for two days and everyone here just wants to drink and feast. This is not the time to be celebrating and it seems everyone forgotten he died. My fiancé Brandle lost his parents at a very young age. I will never really be happy." Onaria turned back around and started falling into the river. "Nooo!" Pon yelled and he quickly grabbed her arm. "Why don't you just let me die? Brandle's body was dumped in this river after he was left lying here dead already. I want to be with him again." "I'm sure he wants you to live for the both of you," Pon said. He pulls her back on her feet. "How can I go on without him?" "You can. Do something nice for yourself. Just don't try to hurt yourself. Come back to the feast with me and start enjoying life again. Pon and Onaria headed back to the feast. Everyone ate as much as they could and danced to some music. Since the feast lasted all day, Joru let Pon and his warriors stay in a vacate cottage for a night, so they could get some good rest before leaving out the next day.

Onaria was up late, alone in her cottage, doing more grieving over Brandle. She was sitting in front of her vanity mirror, trying to wipe off her make-up, but her tears were just making it smear. They've known each other far too long, for her to start over with someone else new. "What will I do now?" She remembered what Pon told her, Do something nice for yourself. Joru and Sile were shaking hands with the brave warriors, the next day. They were about to head back home. "We want to thank you again for what you've done and for staying," Joru said. "Thanks for having us and remember what I said about taking a stand because you never know who can show up at your door," Pon said. "I wonder has Onaria woke up yet? I know she would want to see you all before you leave," Sile said. "Speaking of Onaria … I believe this is her coming," Sheed said. Everyone looked and seen a young woman coming their way. Joru and Sile were shocked on how she looked and so was everybody else. "Hi everyone," Onaria said. "I like the look girl," Sheed said. "Thanks, I like it a lot too." "What's going on? Why did you change your appearance?" Sile asked. "I needed to. Someone told me I needed to do something nice for myself." She looked at Pon. He smiled. "This change will help me get pass my pain." Onaria dyed her hair, shaved it into a mohawk and she had on a fierce looking attire. "And daddy… our people have to learn how to stand up for ourselves. We can't expect others to save us, because next time, it could be too late." "I know darling," Joru said. "Well, it's time for us to head back," Pon said. They climbed on their horses. "Since we all know each other now, we will return. Onaria, if you ever need us, you know where to find us." She saluted them. "Stay brave, brave one," Pon said. Then they all rode off. She watched them until she couldn't see them anymore. She learned a lot from all this… it's not the time to be scared, not anymore.

OUT OF THE VALLEY OF PEACE

Onaria opens a letter that she received from Pon only a month after he and his warriors came to the Valley of Peace. It's been six months since she seen them, but she read the letter many times already. The thought of those warriors crossed her mind, so she had to read that letter once again. The words in that letter warmed her heart and knowing that Pon wrote the letter, because he signed it, and sent it through the telegram. She put the letter back where she kept it, in her drawer. Then Onaria left her cottage to begin her day. She loved taking her walks down to the river. It was something she's been doing every day after Brandle died. Riding the horse was the quicker way to the river, but Onaria preferred to walk there. For the past six months, the men of the village would stand guard of who comes and goes in their village. They even had weapons now to protect the women and children with. Every four hours, they would switch off on a couple different men, so every man can have a chance to guard the village. Some of the men weren't so sure about letting Onaria walk to river by herself. She would tell them she'll be alright. She knew that she would always be alright because it was her place of remembrance of Brandle. But every time she would return to her cottage, Onaria would always feel so alone and grieve. Sile came by to see about her daughter because she's been so worried about her.

"What happened to the lively young woman you use to be?" Sile asked.

"You were always out and about in the village. Now you want to stay cooped up in here and you only want to walk down to the river… which you shouldn't be going there alone. Especially after what happened months ago."

"Mama, you don't understand, I miss him."

"I know, but you have to move on. Brandle would want you to do that."

"I don't know how," Onaria said.

"Stop going down to that river because that's not helping you. That's just keeping the memory of how he died. You should only think about how he lived, how he made you smile. Onaria you are much too young to be living like this. So, get your behind out of this house and be yourself again."

Onaria still wasn't feeling motivated to do anything.

"Well, I'm about to fix your father some dinner. Are you hungry?"

"No, I'm okay," Onaria said.

"You look like you've picked up some weight. Probably because you haven't been that active. Come by if you need us." Sile left. Onaria still chose to sit around in her house and did nothing the rest of day.

When she woke up in the morning, Onaria ate some breakfast, then left her cottage to head down to the river. Once she approached the exit out of the village, the two men on guard were talking to someone, someone that wasn't from their village. It was an elderly man that came by horse. She eased closer to here what the old man was saying. He told the men he traveled such a long distance and needed a place to stop and rest at. The men led the elderly man and his horse into the village. When they all passed her, Onaria wondered where they were taking him to. But she decided to continue on down to the river. Then she was curious of what was going on, so Onaria followed them. It was odd to her that a man his age would be traveling by himself. He looked like he could be in his eighties and could barely walk. The elderly man had a wooden stick that helped him along. He was brought to the leader of their tribe whose name was Serge. Serge was walking through the village when they approached him.

"Sir, we have a visitor… and your name is?" one of the men asked.

"My name is Ethan," the elderly man answered. "I have traveled many miles and the place I called home is longer safe because there was a virus outbreak. Many people have gotten sick and being my age, I could have easily died, so I left."

"So, a virus you say," Serge replied.

"Yes, but I can assure you I didn't catch it because I wouldn't have made it this far. Where I'm from, it's not a very clean place. I think that's why a virus has took over. All I ask is for some place to rest until I know what to do next." Serge looked at the two men. "Give this man something to eat and a place in one of the empty cottages to rest." The two men nodded. "Thank you so much sir," Ethan said, then he followed the men. Onaria stood from a distance and listened to everything that was said.

She went to her parents' cottage to tell them what was going on.

"Mom, Dad, Serge is letting some old man stay here in our village."

"An old man, who is he?" Joru asked.

"His name is Ethan. He traveled a long way from a place where a virus broke out."

"Oh, there isn't a problem, is it?" Sile asked.

"I don't think so, but then I don't know. After what happened six months ago, I don't think we should let outsiders stay in our village."

"You're right, but Serge knows what he's doing. And what harm could one old man do?" Joru asked.

"Yeah, true," Onaria agreed.

"You going down to the river today?" Sile asked.

"No, I have something else to do." Her parents looked at each other. "I'll see you later," Onaria said, as she headed out.

Onaria was keeping an eye on Ethan. He was walking with Serge through the village. Every person passing by Serge introduced Ethan to them and shook hands with them. She stayed out of sight because she wasn't in no hand shaking mood. But then she thought maybe I'm over reacting about this.

Onaria just went back to her cottage and stayed there for the rest of the day.

Everyone was sound asleep by the time midnight rolled around. The night was quiet and still, nothing but the light breeze blowing. Someone decided to come out of their cottage to get a whiff of the night air. Ethan came with the help of his wooden stick to help him walk. He stood for a moment to hear the silence of the night and knew this was the right time to do what he came to the Valley of Peace to do. Ethan began whispering these words, "I have no fear, I won't shed a tear for I have no shame of letting this peaceful place go up in flames." He touched the cottage he was staying in with his wooden stick and a fire arose. Then suddenly each cottage began going up in flames. All the people ran out of their homes. Joru and Sile were out, panicking like everyone else over what just happened and that they couldn't find Onaria among the crowd of people. So, they went to her cottage to see if she was still there. Onaria was in her bed but awoke from the smoke that was coming in her home.

"Onaria! Onaria!" She could hear her mother shout her name from outside. She jumped out of bed, got dressed, and ran out the door. "Onaria… look at what has happened!" Onaria saw that the entire village was in flames.

"This can't be happening," she said. Onaria shut her eyes for a second, then opened them. This was no bad dream. "We should do something. We shouldn't just stand here and watch this," Onaria said.

"What can we do? This is a massive fire," Joru said. Serge gathered fifteen men and they all grabbed a huge water hose from a shed. It took a while for the fire to be put out but got put out.

Everyone has lost sleep over losing their homes but was glad no one was hurt or lost a life. It was devastating that everything they owned was now ashes.

"Now what are we going to do?" Onaria asked.

"Serge says we can rebuild everyone's home," Joru said.

"Does he know what he's saying? That can take a while," Onaria said.

"Living outdoors is not a bad thing, it's beautiful here," Sile said.

"But it gets cold at night," Onaria said.

"We'll still be okay. We still have food and can grow more food and buy more food," Joru said.

"This is not the Valley of Peace anymore. First, we had some invaders, now some old man comes along… where is that man, Ethan?" Onaria asked. She walks around looking at the faces of the people sitting on the ground or standing up and then asked, "Has anyone seen that elderly man that came here yesterday?"

"I don't think no one has seen him since yesterday," a man said. Serge came to her and told her, "That man is nowhere to be found."

"We need to relocate," she told him.

"Why?" Serge asked.

"If we keep staying here, I think something else is going to happen. Twice something has happened… the next time we're not going to be lucky."

"You shouldn't be thinking like that Onaria."

"It seems like I'm the only one that's aware of what's happening," she said. "I don't care what everyone else is planning on doing, I'm leaving the Valley of Peace."

"I'm leaving," she told her parents. "I'm starting over someplace new. You're welcome to come."

"Where are you trying to go?" Sile asked.

"Some place far from here." Onaria looked around at all the people and hopes that everyone hears what she's about to say. "I hope everyone can hear me… I'm leaving the Valley of Peace and if anyone wants to follow me to where I'm going, you're welcome to come along." Everyone looked at each other, then began talking to each other. Onaria and her parents watched all the people talk to each other for the next five minutes. Then everyone stopped.

One man spoke up and said, "We all want to stay here and rebuild our homes." Onaria went to the stables and her parents followed her. She took the palomino horse and grabbed a bag. Then she went to the storage barn and took a few cans of non-perishable food items and some fruit and put them in her bag. She got on the horse, then looked down at Joru and Sile.

"I don't know what you have decided, but I've made my decision… I'm going where the Xene Tribe is."

Onaria and her parents made it to the Xene Tribe's territory the next day. The distance of traveling through the desert was a bit much for Joru and Sile, but they made it through. As they climbed off their horses, they noticed the place was very quiet.

"They must be quiet people," Joru said.

"It's just very early in the morning," Onaria said.

"So, what do we do now? Wait for them to wake up?" Sile asked.

"That's all we can do for now," Onaria answered. They all sat on the ground and waited for the people to wake up from their good night's sleep. Luckily, they were able to get some good sleep on their way there. An hour passed and they haven't seen no one yet. Onaria got up and walked through the Xene Tribe's village to see if anyone was up yet. Someone came out of one of the huts. A woman she remembers named Sheed. "Sheed! Remember me, Onaria?"

"Wow, Onaria… what brings you by so early in the day?"

"I left the Valley of Peace and I have my parents with me. We had a terrible incident that happened in our village that caused us to lose everything including our homes. We just want to start somewhere new. I hope you and your people wouldn't mind if we live here."

"You and your parents are welcomed here. Come, I'll show you where you can stay."

"Let me get my parents." Onaria gets Joru and Sile and Sheed takes them to a little hut that hasn't been occupied in a while.

"Make yourselves at home. Since this is going to be your home now, you can fix it up the way you like. For food you can buy food from some markets that's just walking distance. If you want to make your own food, you can get some non-perishable items from our dry storage that's just down the way. I'll let you all settle in. If you need anything, Onaria you know where to find me."

"Thank you so much," Onaria said. When Sheed was leaving, Onaria thought of something to ask.

"I want to know where Pon is?"

"He's probably on another mission as usual. He usually doesn't come back until past noon. Well, I'll be around if you need me." Onaria and her parents walked down a road to a nearby market where they could buy merchandise. They bought a few items to start off to fix up their new home. Joru and Sile began decorating their place, Onaria wanted to rest so she picked one of the rooms and made it her bedroom. She laid out a pallet and went to sleep.

Onaria woke up two hours later. She smelled something really good in the air. Sile had cooked some hotcakes over a wood burning stove. "How about a late breakfast?" she asked. Onaria sat down at the table and began pouring maple syrup over a plate of hotcakes, her mother sat in front of her. She poured some grape juice in a glass for her. Joru was silently eating his hotcakes.

"So how do you like it in this village so far? Is it some place you would like to stay for a while?"

"It's alright. We'll have to adjust but we haven't really met anyone," Sile said.

"Except for those warriors we met the last time," Joru said.

"I'm going to take a walk through the village," Onaria said after she finished her breakfast. She began walking through the village and saw some people working, children playing and the people just walking by gave her a smile and Onaria smiled back. Further on, she ran into the three teenage girls, Zia, Pinx, and Oma.

"Hi," Zia said. "You're Onaria right?"

"Yes, nice to see you all again."

"We heard you were staying here now," Pinx said.

"Yeah, there was an incident that occurred in my village, so I decided to leave."

"Glad to have you," Oma said.

We're on our way to do some more training on our warrior skills, would you like to come?" Zia asked.

"Maybe next time. Right now, I'm just going to enjoy the walk and get use to a new place."

"Well, we'll see you around," Pinx said. They went on their way and Onaria went her way. Onaria looked at all the houses along the way. Some of the huts were huge and some were smaller. She kept on down the pathway, leading her past more huts. Someone opened their door when Onaria already went past.

"Onaria," someone said. She turned around and it was Pon leaning against his doorway.

She smiled and said, "Pon." She went over to him.

"Where are you heading to?"

"Just walking."

"I'll walk with you." He shuts the door, and they began walking. "So, you're living here now?"

"Yes, I hope that's not a problem."

"No, not at all. What made you want to move here?"

"Everyone's home in our village was destroyed by fire. I believe it was arson. There was an elderly man that came to our village that day it happened. He was allowed to stay in our village because he claimed where he was from, there was a virus outbreak and couldn't go back there. So, the first night he stays in our village, our homes go up in flames. Luckily, no one was hurt."

"Did anyone come here with you?"

"Just my parents. Everyone else wanted to stay in the village to rebuild it. I didn't feel safe there anymore, so I left. First some invaders, then an elderly man is trying to harm us."

"You really think that old man caused the fire?" Pon asked.

"I can't prove it and it's kind of unreal that he could of did it, but he had to have help and this did happen in the middle of the night."

"He might of came from the same place those unwanted guests came from and they probably helped him too," Pon said.

"Maybe," she agreed. They quit talking for a moment and just kept walking. "Oh, about the letter you wrote," Onaria began, "That was very nice of you."

"I was hoping you was going to bring the subject up," he said. "Why don't we talk about this more this evening. Let's have dinner by the river about seven."

"Oh, a date?" Onaria asked.

"Yeah," he said.

"Okay."

Pon came by Onaria's place that evening. He had already picked up something for the both of them to eat and he had it in a basket. They picked a comfortable spot by the river and a great spot to see the sun before it set. They both changed into something comfortable for their date because it was such a warm evening. They laid out a blanket to sit on. Then Pon started taking food out of the basket. He began feeding her some things that had a kick to it and some did not, but Onaria liked what he was feeding her even though she had no idea what she was eating.

"What is this that I'm eating?"

"It's mush. Mashed up mushrooms that was baked with flavoring in it." They also ate baked salmon. Onaria thought it was very good but have eaten salmon a few times before. They drank some wine for this fancy occasion.

"This was nice of you to do this," Onaria said.

"I thought a lot about you ever since we've met," Pon said.

"Really?"

"Yes," he answered.

"I have to admit, I've been thinking about you too." He stared at her, and she stared at him. Onaria felt herself getting a little warm but needed an excuse to go back home by saying, "I think we should leave before the mosquitos come out."

"What? We did just get here."

"Please." They packed up everything and Pon walked her home. Before Onaria went inside, she said, "I enjoyed myself this evening. I hope we can do this again."

"Sure," he said, "I enjoyed myself too." He stared at her again and she could feel herself getting warmer.

"Goodnight," she said to him, and she went inside.

Onaria had just opened the door the next morning and Pon was outside standing there. "Oh Pon, hi… nice to see you again this morning."

"I just wanted to see you before I leave… I have to do some lumbering."

"Ok." They began walking. "I have to start off saying… you're a nice-looking man."

"Thank you, you're a beautiful woman."

"Are you dating any of the women here in the village?"

"No, because I'm always gone on missions so I could never have a serious relationship with anyone, at least not anymore. Sheed and I use to use to date, but she's married now."

"Oh really," she said.

"Yeah," he said.

"Well, this is hard for me, dating someone new. I've been with the last man for so long. Even though it's been months since he's been here."

"It's nothing wrong with starting over Onaria. You and I can just be friends if you want… "

"Yes, just friends," she said.

"Well, I have to go… I'll see you tomorrow," Pon said.

"Ok, I'll see you tomorrow."

Pon, Rageed, and Conod were chopping up wood in a forest outside of their village. They were going into the fall season and the nights have been way cooler now. The wood was for everyone in the village and the fireplaces in their homes. The men spent a couple hours working and now they needed a break. There was an area that was walking distance, where there were bars. This is where the three of them frequently came to. They would get their liquor and then head next door to this dark place where there were voluptuous women. The women would get paid up front, then they would engage in sexual activities with them. This was something Pon, Rageed, and Conod have been doing for years. But this was not the day Pon was interested in any woman he didn't have any idea what their name was. While Rageed and Conod were having sex with their women, Pon was just staring at his lady. She was just standing in front of him, topless with only thongs on. They kept staring at each other, but she was wondering when the action was going to begin. Pon was imagining Onaria standing here instead of the prostitute.

"Is something wrong?" she asked.

"No, just not in the mood," he answered. He left the building. Rageed stopped in the middle of having sex and yelled out, "Pon, where are you going?" Conod stopped too, wondering what was going on.

Onaria was with Sheed and a few other young women, learning some warrior skills in the afternoon, the next day. Onaria didn't think she was that great at learning how to be a warrior. She never thought she would be doing this. Onaria was glad when the lesson was over for the day.

"Don't worry, you'll get the hang of it," Sheed told her before she headed back home. Just when Onaria arrived at her place, she saw Pon coming her way. He had a wheelbarrow full of chopped wood.

"Hi," she said, and he said, "hi. I bought some wood for your fireplace. You're going to need it for these cold nights."

"Yes, thank you." Onaria opened the door for him, and he picked up a few of the wood logs and they went inside. Joru and Sile were eating lunch at their table. Pon spoke to them, and they spoke back.

"I bought some wood for your fireplace."

"Thank you, young man," Joru said. He sat the wood logs on the floor by the fireplace.

"If you ever need anything else, don't hesitate to find me," Pon said.

"We will let you know," Sile said.

"You folks have a nice day." Pon took Onaria by the hand, wanting her to come outside with him. Once they were outside, he put both his hands upon her shoulders. "How would you feel about having a date night at my place tonight?"

"Another date? Are you cooking?"

"Yes, I don't mind cooking for you," he answered.

"That would be nice," she said.

"I won't be back home until after dark, but I'll have everything ready. Just be there at my place before I get back home."

"I will," she promised.

"I'll see you tonight," he said before he walked away.

Wow, Onaria thought to herself, he is so hot, it's making me hot.

Onaria dressed up for the occasion, not too fancy, but she wanted to look nice. The evenings had gotten cooler, so she wrapped herself in a shawl. Once she entered in his house, Onaria couldn't believe how unique it looked. It was spacious, very dim lit which made his place look romantic like and the carpet was so soft, your feet sunk in it. The color of the carpet was beautiful, it was cream color and fuzzy. She took her shoes off, thinking Pon probably didn't want no one to wear shoes on his carpet. Onaria wondered how many women has he brought here? It did look like a bachelor's pad. It smelled good in his place because of whatever he cooked was sitting on his stove, but the stove was not on. Nothing to do at the moment, but to sit and wait for Pon. So, she sat on the floor and how comfortable it was. He had chairs, but the floor seemed better to sit on. The fireplace was going, which made his place cozy. The sun has went down and an hour has passed, but Pon hasn't come home yet. Onaria was staring at the fire in the fireplace. Then she felt sleepy and laid down on the soft fuzzy carpet.

Onaria was asleep then heard a voice in her ear saying, "Wake up sweet thang."

She opened her eyes and Pon was there. Onaria sat up and said, "Oh, Pon I almost forgot where I was… I dosed off."

"That's okay," he said. He was sitting next to her. "I got something for us." He had a bottle of wine. "I hope you brought an appetite because dinner's almost ready."

"Yes, but right now I'd like an appetizer." She wrapped her arms around him and began kissing him. He was kissing her back then they ended up naked, making love on the floor. Onaria sunk down in the carpet, while Pon was on top of her. She thought he felt so good inside her and how strong he was. Onaria wrapped her legs around him as he continued to pound her. Then she got on top of him, and he was loving every minute of that. The next position, he made love to her from the back. Then they paused for a moment. Onaria leaned against a chair while still sitting on the floor. Pon popped open the wine bottle he bought and poured some wine on her chest. He sat the wine bottle down and then started licking up the wine off her breast in a circular motion. Then he was licking the wine that ran down to her naval, next he was making his way down in between her legs. Onaria had to stop him.

"What's wrong?" he asked.

"I can't get into oral sex," she said. "I know you're going to want me to do the same to you. I don't know how many women you have put your penis into."

"Well, I believe in pleasuring a woman… I like to go all the way."

"I can't let you go that way on me." Pon was disappointed.

"I'm sorry, I didn't mean to upset you."

"I'm not upset." Onaria knew he was upset because Pon was looking down at the floor and being quiet. She rubbed up against him and then started to stroke his penis. Just something to make him feel good all over again. Then she climbed on him and really put it on him.

Pon and Onaria ate dinner then laid down under a blanket.

"How did you learn to cook so well?" she asked.

"From the women in my family. Basically, everything I learned was from a woman."

"Have you always been going on missions?"

"Yes, for many years. That's why I haven't been in a relationship for so long."

"So, do you just chop down trees or do you do other kind of work on your missions?" Before Pon could answer, a knock was at the door. He picked up a towel and wrapped it around his waist, then went to the door.

Pon, are you alright?" Rageed asked. "Me and Conod didn't know what to think when you walked out of the place yesterday. Then I thought maybe he's tired of the scene. There's another spot where there's all kinds of women."

"Rageed, now's not the time, it's late."

"What's your plan tomorrow? Is it at the same spot?" Rageed asked.

"My plan is to stay home. I'm taking a break from that," Pon said.

"Fine by me. Just wanted to check on ya."

"I'm good," Pon said. Rageed left and Pon shut the door. Onaria had listened to their conversation and wasn't too thrilled about what she heard. Pon got back under the blanket with her. "So, what were we talking about?" he asked.

"So, are you dating other women?" Onaria asked.

"What are you talking about?"

"You didn't think I heard what you and Rageed were talking about?"

"Yeah, we go on missions, we work."

"So, is finding women part of the job too?" She moved away from him. "Are you picking up prostitutes?"

"Come on, they don't mean anything to me," Pon said.

"Answer the question."

"Yes… but I'm not trying to do that anymore." Onaria jumped up and got dressed.

"What are you doing Onaria?"

"It's time for me to leave."

"It's late and you shouldn't walk alone."

"I'll be alright," she said, and she left.

Sile and Joru were sitting at their kitchen table. They had just finished eating breakfast and Sile opened up a letter she had just received. "It's from Serge," she said.

"What's he saying?" Joru asked.

"All is well," she began reading, "The rebuilding of the village is coming along very quickly. Everyone has been working together. We want you to come back so we can help you rebuild your home. It will be better than before. Another thing…remember that elderly man, Ethan that was passing through that needed a place to live? Well, he returned a few days ago. We questioned his absence and he said he had to return home to check on some family members. I remember him saying he couldn't go back home because of some virus outbreak. During his stay back here, some of our people had become sick behind some food they ate. We all know none of our people have ever got sick because of food poisoning. One night someone caught Ethan in the food barn contaminating our food supply by putting drops of animal blood in the food. He's also the one that tried to destroy our homes by arson. We have him held in captive and managed to get the truth out of him of how he started the fire… he used some magic spell. Why did he do this? We don't know but thanks to some great medicine, the people had recovered from the food poisoning. We want you to come back, we miss you, Serge."

"Wow, what do you think? Should we go back?" Joru asked.

"I think we should. I'm homesick anyway. Onaria should know about this. She's probably still asleep," Sile said. She gets up and goes to Onaria's room. "Onaria… are you still asleep?"

"No, I'm awake." Onaria was lying down in her bed, but had her back towards Sile.

"When are you getting up?"

"I want to stay in bed today. I didn't get any sleep last night."

"Well, me and your father have to make a run. We'll be back in a little bit. We also have some great news you might want to hear when we get back." She didn't want to hear anything but quietness. That's what she got once her parents left. Then a few minutes later, someone was knocking at the front door. Onaria was going to ignore whoever it was at the door but got up anyway. When she opened the door, she wasn't surprised that it was Pon.

"Can we talk?" he asked.

"There's really nothing to talk about, Pon."

"I want to explain." She let him in. They sat at the kitchen table. They were sitting across from each other. Pon was looking at her, but Onaria was looking elsewhere with her arms folded. "Onaria, I want to be with you and only you."

"But you mess around with prostitutes."

"I use to. Now I've decided not to do that anymore. I didn't know I was going to meet you and have these feelings about you. I wouldn't do anything to hurt you. I'm not doing any work today. I'm going to be here all day and I would like to spend it with you. I'll be nearby if you need me. He gets up and leaves. Onaria was still sitting at the kitchen table only caring about her quiet time. Then she notices a piece of paper on the table. She reads it and says, "This is what my mother wants to talk about."

Sile and Joru came back thirty minutes later. "So, are you planning on going back to the Valley of Peace?" Onaria asked.

"Yes, I told Serge in a telegram I just sent that we will be returning," Sile said.

"Do you want to go back home?" Joru asked Onaria.

"I guess I do," Onaria answered.

"I know you've gotten used to being here… but the choice is yours my dear," Sile said.

"Yeah, I'll think about it," she said.

Serge had sent a telegram later that day to them. He told them that they were going to be flown back by plane in the next couple of days to save them the trouble of traveling long distance by horse. Onaria didn't go by

Pon's place until the next day, but he wasn't there. She looked around most of the village as she could but still didn't run into him. Onaria and her parents had got the word out that they were heading back to the Valley of Peace tomorrow morning. They had packed all their things that night. Sile and Joru had gone straight to sleep but Onaria still had trouble sleeping. She wasn't too thrilled about going back home as they were.

Tomorrow had come very quickly. Serge had flown in with two other men by afternoon. They had a second plane so Sile, Joru and Onaria could load their horses on. Serge gave Sile and Joru big hugs when they finally seen each other. Onaria was still unsure about going back, so she wasn't leaping for joy. Some of the people of the village was there to see them off. "We're going to miss you guys," Sheed said to Onaria.

"I'm going to miss you all too," Onaria said. Oma, Pinx, and Zia were there with sad looks on their faces. Out of the blue, Pon shows up.

"Onaria wait!" He tries to catch his breath from running so fast. "I wanted to see you last night, but it was so late. So, you leaving?"

"Yes I am."

"Is that what you really want to?"

"What do you mean?"

"I thought you liked it here."

"I do."

"It's a long distance between your home and mine… and I don't believe in long distance affairs," he said.

"I don't either," Onaria said.

"Then stay." She walked away. Her parents were already on the plane and Onaria got on the plane too. Pon know now it's over between them. She didn't say good-bye because she's probably still mad, he thought to himself. He started walking back to his house. The two planes have taken off, but Pon could hear the crowd of people, sounding happy. He stopped and turned around. Onaria was still here, talking to Sheed and other people. Pon was shocked and he went back. Pon and Onaria stared at each other. "What happened?" he asked.

"I told my parents that I love them, and I will always write to them. I want to also leave the painful memory of my fiancé behind." Pon had his arms out. She ran to him, and they hugged each other. Everyone went about their business so they could be alone. Pon and Onaria kept on hugging each other because ever since they met, they never wanted to let each other go.

THE END

ABOUT THE AUTHOR

Embark on a thrilling journey through imaginative worlds with Tamara Barnett, born in Longview, Texas in 1976. Though a new author, her passion for writing spans years. From her debut in 2017 with "Religion, Romance, and Real Life", to the captivating "Seasons of Love to Deep South Love" in 2023, Tamara surely has mesmerized readers. Now, in 2024, she ventures into science fiction with "Another World, Another Place". Join her on this odyssey, where mysteries collide with the human spirit. Expect many more great books from Tamara!

www.ingramcontent.com/pod-product-compliance
Lightning Source LLC
Chambersburg PA
CBHW071433300726
48976CB00004B/1322